Bella bit her lip, suddenly unsure about what she should do.

Should she break the contact, step away from him and make it clear that she didn't welcome this kind of intimacy? But surely that would be a lie? Having Mac hold her, caress her, make her feel all those things, *was* what she wanted.

Desperately.

Helplessly, her eyes rose to his, and she felt her heart lurch when she saw the awareness on his face. She knew in that moment that Mac understood how confused she felt because he felt the same. Whether or not it was that thought—that single mind-blowing thought—that unlocked all her reservations, she didn't pause to consider what she was doing as she reached up and drew his head down. Their mouths met, clung, and it was like nothing she had experienced before. There was desire, yes, but there was so much more to the kiss than passion. The feel of Mac's mouth on hers made her feel safe, secure, protected.

It was as though she had found her way back home after a long and exhausting journey.

Dear Reader,

Should best friends fall in love? That is the question that both Bella and Mac ask themselves after they meet again following Bella's divorce. Their relationship was so clear in the past: they were friends and nothing more than that. However, all of a sudden they find their feelings for one another changing.

It comes as a huge shock to Mac. After all, he's convinced that Bella is to blame for the demise of her marriage. But the more time they spend together, the harder he finds it to believe that. As for Bella—well, she has never been good at relationships. She has always had great difficulty showing her feelings, so to suddenly discover just how hard it is to remain emotionally detached when Mac is around scares her. After all, she doesn't have a good track record when it comes to relationships, does she? Even if it *was* her ex-husband's fault that their marriage failed. Is it realistic to hope that she and Mac can switch from being friends to lovers?

Helping Bella and Mac work through their problems was a real pleasure. I grew extremely fond of them during the course of writing this book. They deserve to find happiness after everything they've been through, and I hope you will agree that they truly earn their happy ending.

Best wishes to you all

Jennifer

To learn more about the writing of this book do visit my blog: jennifertaylorauthor.wordpress.com.

BEST FRIEND TO PERFECT BRIDE

BY
JENNIFER TAYLOR

First published in Great Britain 2015
By Mills & Boon, an imprint of HarperCollins*Publishers*
1 London Bridge Street, London, SE1 9GF

Large Print edition 2016

© 2015 Jennifer Taylor

ISBN: 978-0-263-26076-2

Printed and bound in Great Britain
by CPI Antony Rowe, Chippenham, Wiltshire

Jennifer Taylor has been writing Mills & Boon novels for some time, but discovered Medical Romance books relatively recently. She was so captivated by these heartwarming stories that she immediately set out to write them herself! Having worked in scientific research, Jennifer enjoys writing each book, as well as the chance to create a cast of wonderful new characters. Jennifer's hobbies include reading and travelling. She lives in northwest England. Visit Jennifer's blog at jennifertaylorauthor.wordpress.com.

Books by Jennifer Taylor

Mills & Boon Medical Romance

The Doctor's Baby Bombshell
The Midwife's Christmas Miracle
Small Town Marriage Miracle
Gina's Little Secret
The Family Who Made Him Whole
The Son That Changed His Life
The Rebel Who Loved Her
The Motherhood Mix-Up
Mr Right All Along
Saving His Little Miracle
One More Night with Her Desert Prince...

Visit the Author Profile page at millsandboon.co.uk for more titles.

For Charlotte, who told me about the boat
Gallina, and for James, who owns her.
Many thanks for providing me with
the perfect home for my hero.

CHAPTER ONE

SHE HADN'T CHANGED. Tall and slender, her red-gold hair coiled into an elegant knot at the nape of her neck, Bella English looked as beautiful today as she had done the last time he had seen her. On her wedding day.

'Mac! I heard you were back. Good to see you, mate. How are you?'

'Great, thanks, Lou.'

James MacIntyre—Mac to all who knew him—turned and grinned at the elderly porter. Out of the corner of his eye he saw Bella move away from the desk but he kept his attention firmly focused on the other man. After what his old friend Tim had told him, he wasn't all that eager to speak to her.

'You're looking well, I must say, Lou. Obviously, moving to the new paediatric A&E unit has done you the power of good. You look a good ten years younger than the last time I saw you!'

'I wish!' Lou's grizzled face broke into a wry smile. 'It'd take major surgery to turn me into Dalverston's very own version of George Clooney.' He glanced over Mac's shoulder and grimaced. 'Anyway, I'd better get going. Catch you later.'

'Yep.'

Mac didn't need to check to see what had caused Lou to beat a hasty retreat. He could smell her perfume, that subtle fragrance of freesias that Bella always wore. She had told him once that it was made especially for her and that had fitted perfectly with everything he knew about her. Bella was the sort of woman who would have her very own perfume. Nothing about her was ordinary or commonplace.

Mac turned slowly around, taking stock of all the details he had missed before. Although Bella had always been slender, she was verging on thin now, he realised. And even though her complexion was as creamy as ever, there were dark circles under her green eyes that hinted at far too many sleepless nights. Was it guilt that had kept her awake? he wondered a shade bitterly. A noisy conscience clamouring to be heard, even if it was too late in the day? After all, even Bella must feel some degree of remorse about ending her marriage to Tim.

'Hello, Mac. I heard you were back. How are you?'

The greeting was almost identical to Lou's, but Mac had to admit that it made him want to respond very differently. He experienced an uncharacteristic urge to take her by the shoulders and shake her, demand to know why she had done such a cruel thing. She had ruined Tim's life—didn't she care? Didn't she care either that she had broken all those promises she had made three years ago to love, honour and cherish the man she had married? He had sat through the ceremony, listened to her cool clear voice swearing a lifetime's devotion, and had believed every word. If he was honest, he felt almost as let down as poor Tim must do.

The thought shocked him so that it was a moment before he answered. He and Bella had never been anything more than friends—he had made sure of that. So why should he feel so disillusioned? He blanked out the thought, knowing it was foolish to dwell on it. If he and Bella were to work together for the next few months, he couldn't allow recent events to stand in the way.

'Fine, thanks. Looking forward to working in the new unit.' He glanced around and nodded. 'It looks great, I must say. Obviously, no expense has been spared.'

'No. Everything is state of the art. We've

been open for almost a month now and I still have to pinch myself when I come into work. I can't believe that we have such marvellous facilities to hand.'

She gave a husky laugh and Mac tensed when he felt the tiny hairs all over his body spring to attention. He had forgotten about her laugh, forgotten how soft it was, how *sexy*. It had been her laugh that he had noticed first, in fact. He had been standing in the lunch queue in the university's refectory when he had heard a woman laugh and he had turned to see who it was…

He ditched that thought as well, not needing any more distractions. He knew where his loyalties lay, knew that if he had to take sides then he would be firmly allied to Tim. Tim had poured out the whole sorry tale, told him what had happened from start to finish, and whilst Mac was realistic enough to know that it was rarely all one person's fault when a marriage ended, it was obvious that Bella was more at fault than Tim. No, Tim's biggest mistake had been to love Bella too much and be too soft with her. The thought firmed his resolve and he smiled thinly at her.

'Is that what brought you to Dalverston, the chance to work in a wonderful new facility like this? I must confess that I was surprised to learn you had moved out of London.'

'It was one of the reasons, yes.'

Bella's expression sobered and Mac's heart twisted when he saw the pain in her eyes. Maybe Tim *was* hurting but Bella was hurting too, it seemed. The idea affected him far more than it should have done, far more than he wanted it to do. It was an effort not to let her see how he felt when she continued.

'I needed to get away and moving up here seemed like the right thing to do. It's a fresh start for me and, hopefully, it will be a fresh start for Tim as well.'

* * *

Bella could feel the animosity coming off Mac in huge waves and it hurt to know that he had judged her and obviously found her wanting. She knew that Tim would have told Mac his version of the story but she had hoped that Mac would wait until he had spoken to her before he started apportioning blame. However, it appeared that he had accepted what Tim had said without question. *She* was the one at fault, the bad guy who had called time on her marriage, while Tim was the innocent victim.

She swung round, refusing to stand there and try to justify herself. She had made up her mind that she wouldn't retaliate after she had found out that Tim had been spreading all those lies about her. She had seen that happen with other couples, had watched as the situation had deteriorated into an unseemly sparring match, and she had sworn that she wouldn't go down that route. People would believe what they wanted to believe anyway. If she tried to contest Tim's claims that she had been unreasonable, that she had ruined his career, that she had ended their relationship rather than have a baby with him, few would believe her.

She had always been the reticent one in the relationship, the one who took longer to make friends, whereas Tim had always been very outgoing. Tim drew people to him and made instant friends of them, and if he tended to drop them just as quickly later, then nobody seemed to mind. No, if there were sides to be taken then most folk would take Tim's. Including Mac, it seemed.

Pain stabbed her heart as she led the way to Reception. Even though she knew it was silly, she hated to think that she had sunk so low in Mac's estimation. Dredging up a smile, she turned to Janet Davies, their receptionist, determined that she wasn't going to let him know how she felt.

'This is Dr MacIntyre, Janet. He'll be covering the senior registrar's post until Dr Timpson is fit to return to work following her accident.'

'Oh, I know Mac. Who doesn't?' Janet got up and hurried around the desk to give Mac a hug. She grinned up at him. 'So where was it this time? Africa? India? Outer Mongolia?'

'The Philippines.'

Mac hugged Janet back, his face breaking into a smile that immediately warmed Bella's heart. He had always had the most wonderful smile, she thought, then pulled herself up short. Maybe Mac had smiled at Janet with genuine warmth but he certainly hadn't smiled at her that way.

'Oh, grim.' Janet grimaced. 'Was it as bad as it looked on TV?'

'Worse.'

Mac shook his head, his dark brown hair

flopping untidily across his forehead. It needed trimming, Bella decided, even though it suited him, emphasising his craggy good looks and that air of toughness he projected. Mac looked exactly like the kind of man he was: tough, unflappable, someone you could depend on, someone who would never let you down. Her heart ached even harder at the thought. She could have done with Mac's support this past difficult year.

'The typhoon destroyed whole cities and left people with nothing except the clothes they stood up in. We had a devil of a job getting hold of even the most basic supplies in the be-ginning,' he continued.

'How awful!' Janet shuddered as she went back to her seat. 'Makes you grateful that you live here, doesn't it.'

'It does indeed.' Mac grinned. 'Even if it does rain a lot in this part of the world!'

Janet laughed as she reached for the telephone when it started ringing. Bella moved to the whiteboard and checked the list of names written on it, determined to start as she meant to go on. Maybe there were certain issues that she and Mac needed to address, but they were colleagues, first and foremost, and she intended to keep that at the forefront of her mind. There were just three children in cubicles and each of them had been seen and were currently awaiting the results of various tests. She pointed to the last name on the list when Mac joined her.

'I'd like you to take a look at this one, if you wouldn't mind. Chloe Adams, aged eight, admitted at four a.m. this morning complaining of a severe headache. She'd also been vomiting.' She sighed. 'Apparently, she's been suffering from violent headaches for several weeks. Mum took her to their GP, who thought it was probably a sinus infection, but I'm not convinced.'

'So what are you thinking?' Mac queried. 'That it's something more sinister?'

'Yes. I noticed a definite lack of coordination when I was examining her. It made me wonder if it's a tumour. I asked Mum if she'd noticed anything—clumsy gait, frequent falls, that kind of thing—but she said she hadn't.' Bella shrugged. 'Chloe is one of five children and I get the impression that her mother is finding it hard to cope since their father upped and left them at the beginning of the year.'

'I see. It must be difficult for her when she's been abandoned like that,' Mac said blandly, so blandly in fact that Bella knew he was thinking about her situation.

Colour touched her cheeks as she led the way to the cubicles. She hadn't abandoned Tim! She had left because Tim had made it impossible for her to stay. She had tried to help him, tried everything she could think of, but nothing had worked. He had been too dependent on the painkillers by then to give them up. Oh, he had promised that he would, swore that he had umpteen times, but he had lied. The drugs had changed him from the man she had married, turned him into someone who lied and deceived at the drop of a hat. It had reached the point where she simply couldn't take any more and she had left and, amazingly, it had been the best thing she could have done for him.

Tim had sought help after that. He had admitted himself to rehab and finally kicked his habit. Maybe she should have gone back to him then—she had thought about it. But then she had found out about his affair and there hadn't seemed any point. She would only have gone back out of a sense of duty and that hadn't seemed right or fair to either of them.

It made her wonder all of a sudden if she had ever really loved him—loved him with the depth and intensity that people were supposed to feel when they married—if she hadn't been prepared to fight for him. The problem was that she had never been truly in touch with her feelings. As the only child of career-minded parents, she had learned at an early age to keep her emotions in check. Even after she had grown up, she had always held back, had always been wary about letting herself feel. Tim had seemed like a safe bet—the type of man she was used to, someone from her own social circle, someone she felt comfortable with. Unlike Mac. Mac had been very different. Even though they'd only been friends, his self-assurance and experience of life had unsettled her. Everything about him had seemed alien. Dangerous. A threat to her peace of mind. He still was.

Bella's breath caught. If Mac had seemed dangerous all those years ago, he was even more of a threat now that she was so vulnerable.

'Mrs Adams? I'm Dr MacIntyre. Dr English has asked me to take a look at your daughter.'

Mac smiled at the harassed-looking woman sitting beside the bed. He knew that Bella was standing right behind him and forced himself to focus on the other woman. He had sworn that he would behave with the utmost propriety and wouldn't take Bella to task about what she had done. Maybe he *did* believe that she had behaved deplorably by ending her marriage, but it wasn't his place to say so.

'She's feeling a lot better now, aren't you, Chloe?' Donna Adams turned to the little girl, urging her to agree, and Mac sighed. No matter how long this took or how inconvenient it was for the mother, they needed to get to the bottom of Chloe's problem.

'That's good to hear but I still think it would be best if we carried out a couple more tests.' He smiled at the little girl. 'We don't want you having any more of those horrible headaches if we can avoid it, do we, Chloe?'

'No.' She smiled shyly back at him, clutching tight hold of a battered old teddy bear.

Mac grinned at her as he sat down on the edge of the bed. 'What's your teddy's name? I have a bear just like him and he's called Bruno.'

'William.' Chloe gave the bear a hug. 'He's my best friend and I take him everywhere.'

'I expect he enjoys it.' Mac took hold of the bear's paw and solemnly shook it. 'It's nice to meet you, William. My name's Dr Mac.'

Chloe giggled at this piece of nonsense, but Mac knew that it was important to gain her trust. He smiled at her again. 'So, now the introductions are over, I need to ask you some questions, Chloe. There are no right or wrong answers, mind you. And if you want William to help you then that's also fine. OK?'

'OK,' Chloe agreed happily.

'So, Chloe, have you noticed that sometimes

you don't seem quite as steady on your feet as normal and fall over?'

'Sometimes,' Chloe murmured. She glanced at her mother then hurried on. 'It happened in school the other day. I got up to fetch a piece of paper to do some painting and fell over. Teacher thought I was messing about and told me off.'

'I see.' Mac glanced at Bella and saw her nod. Poor balance could point towards a disturbance to the function of the cerebellum and was often an indication of a tumour. Although he hoped with all his heart it wasn't that, it was looking increasingly likely.

'And have you found it difficult to walk sometimes, as though your feet don't want to do what you tell them to?' he continued gently.

'Yes. Sometimes they keep going the wrong way,' Chloe told him guilelessly.

'I'm sorry, Doctor, but what has this got to

do with Chloe's headaches?' Donna Adams demanded.

'It all helps to build up a picture of what might be wrong with Chloe,' Mac explained, not wanting to go into detail just yet. If their suspicions were correct then there would be time enough for the poor woman to face the fact that her child was seriously ill. He stood up and smiled at Chloe. 'I'm going to send you for a special scan, Chloe, so we can see what's happening inside your head. I just need to make a phone call first and then the porter will take you and your mum downstairs to have it done.'

'Will it take long?' Donna Adams asked anxiously. 'Only I've got to get the others ready for school. They're with my neighbour at the moment but I can't expect her to see to them. She's in her eighties and it's far too much for her.'

'The scan itself won't take very long,' Bella said gently. 'However, Chloe will need to stay

here until we get the results back. Is there anyone else you can contact who could see to the
children?'

'No.' Donna's tone was bitter. 'There's nobody
since their dad upped and left.' She glanced at
her daughter and sighed. 'They'll just have to
miss school today, I suppose.'

Mac didn't say anything as he followed Bella
from the cubicle, but it didn't mean that he
wasn't thinking it. Breaking promises was a definite no-no in his view. He only had to recall his
own father's despair after his mother had walked
out on them to know that it was something he
would never do. If he ever made a commitment
then he would stick to it, no matter what.

He glanced at Bella and could tell from her
expression that she knew what he was thinking, but it was hard luck. Letting Tim down the
way she had was beyond the pale, in his opinion. She had promised to love and cherish Tim
for the rest of her days but she hadn't meant

it. She couldn't have done if at the first sign of trouble she had turned her back on him. He felt guilty enough about not being there when Tim had needed his support, even though he'd had no idea what his friend had been going through. However, Bella *had* been there and, as Tim's wife, she should have been the one person he could rely on. It was little wonder that his friend was so devastated.

Mac's mouth thinned as he followed her into the office. Maybe it was unfair of him to be so judgemental but he had always considered Bella to be the ideal woman. Not only was she beautiful, but she was highly intelligent too. Although he had been deeply attracted to her when they had met at Cambridge, he had been ever so slightly in awe of her as well. The fact that she had kept herself aloof from the rest of their class had only added to her allure, in fact.

He had never been the reticent type. His upbringing, on a council estate on the outskirts of

Manchester, hadn't allowed for such luxury. He had learned early on that he needed to be tough to survive, focused and determined if he hoped to achieve his goal of becoming a doctor. Bella had been very different from the girls he had known at home, different too from the rest of the women in their year at university. Although many of them had come from privileged backgrounds too, Bella had stood out: her perfection had made her special. To discover that she wasn't perfect after all had hit him hard. For all these years he had put her on a pedestal but the truth was that Bella was just a woman like any other, a woman who could make and break promises. She wasn't special. And she wasn't out of his league, as he had always believed.

Mac frowned. It was the first time that thought had crossed his mind and he didn't like it. Not one little bit. Or the one that followed it. There was nothing to stop him making a play for Bella now.

* * *

Sadly, the results of Chloe's scan only confirmed their suspicions. Bella sighed as she studied the monitor. 'There's no doubt about it, is there? That's definitely a tumour.'

'It is.'

Mac leant forward to get a better look and she tensed when his shoulder brushed against hers. She moved aside, not enjoying the fact that her heart seemed to be beating far faster than it normally did. She cleared her throat. The last thing she needed was Mac thinking that he had any kind of effect on her.

'It's probably a medulloblastoma, wouldn't you say? That's one of the most common types of brain tumour that occur in children.'

'Oh, yes. The fact that it's arisen in the cerebellum makes it almost a certainty,' he concurred.

'Chloe's going to need immediate treatment,' Bella said, focusing on their patient in the hope that it would stop her thoughts wandering again. Maybe she did seem to be unusually aware of Mac, but that was only to be expected. Ever since she'd heard he was back in England, she had been on edge. After all, Mac was Tim's best friend and it must be hard for him to accept what had happened. It was bound to lead to a certain degree of…well, *tension* between them. The thought was reassuring and she hurried on.

'From what I've read, medulloblastomas can grow very rapidly and spread to other parts of the brain as well as to the spinal cord.'

'That's right. Chloe needs to be seen by an oncologist ASAP so we shall have to set that up. She'll probably need radiotherapy as well as chemotherapy if she's to have any chance of surviving this.' He shook his head and Bella saw the sorrow in his eyes. 'I feel sorry for her mother. It's going to be a huge shock for her.'

'It will be a lot for her to deal with, especially

with having the other children to look after,'
Bella agreed quietly. 'Just travelling back and
forth to hospital while Chloe receives treatment will be a major task with her not having
any backup.'

'It will.'

Mac's tone was flat. Although there was no
hint of censure in his voice, Bella knew that
he was thinking about the way she had seem-
ingly deserted Tim in his hour of need. The
urge to tell him the truth—the *real* truth, not
the version that Tim was determined to tell
everyone—was very strong but she refused to
go down that path. It wouldn't improve Mac's
opinion of her if she tried to apportion blame;
it could have the opposite effect, in fact.

It was hard to accept that there was very
little she could do, but Bella knew there was
no point agonising about it. Switching off the
monitor, she turned to leave the office. 'I'll
go and have a word with Mrs Adams,' she

said over her shoulder. 'The sooner she knows what's going on, the better.'

'Fine. Do you want me to phone Oncology and start the ball rolling?' Mac offered, following her out to the corridor.

'If you wouldn't mind… Oh, they've got a new phone number. They're starting the refurbishments today so they've moved temporarily into the old building. I'll get it for you.' Bella went to go back into the office and staggered when she cannoned into Mac.

'Sorry.' He grinned as he set her safely back on her feet. 'I didn't expect you to turn round so suddenly, or that's my excuse, anyway. It's got nothing whatsoever to do with me being born clumsy!'

'No harm done,' she assured him, although she could feel heat flowing from the point where his hands were gripping her shoulders. She stepped back, setting some much-needed space between them, or much-needed by her, at least. Mac appeared unmoved by the contact. 'Janet should have Oncology's new number, now that I think about it,' she said, hastily squashing that thought. 'Let me know what they say, won't you?'

'Will do.'

He sketched her a wave as he headed to Reception. Bella watched until he disappeared from sight then made her way to the cubicles. She wasn't looking forward to the next few minutes. Breaking bad news to a parent was always difficult and one of the few things she disliked about her job…

Her breath caught as she felt the heat finally consume her entire body. It felt as though she was on fire, burning up, inside and out, and all because Mac had touched her. She couldn't recall ever feeling this way before, couldn't remember when the touch of a man's hands had set her alight, not even when Tim had made love to her. What did it mean? Or didn't it mean anything really? Was it simply the lack of intimacy that had made her so susceptible all of a sudden?

Once Tim had become hooked on the pain-killers, they had stopped making love. He hadn't been interested in anything apart from where his next fix was coming from and she hadn't been able to stand the thought of them being intimate when it wouldn't have meant anything. It was almost two years since they had slept together and there had been nobody else since, or at least not for her. Was that why she felt so aware of her body all of a sudden, so emotionally charged? It wasn't Mac's touch per se that had aroused her but the fact that she had been denied an outlet for her feelings for such a long time?

Bella told herself that it was the real explanation; however, as she entered the cubicle, she knew in her heart that it was only partly true. Maybe the lack of intimacy was a contributing factor but she doubted if she would have reacted this way if another man had touched her the way Mac had done. The truth was that she had always been aware of him even though they had never been anything more than friends. There was something about him that she responded to, even though she had refused to acknowledge it. It made her see just how careful she needed to be. The last thing she wanted was to start craving Mac's touch when it was obvious how he felt about her.

CHAPTER TWO

IT WAS A busy day but Mac enjoyed every second. Although he had worked in emergency medicine for some time, paediatric emergency care on this scale was a whole new ball game. The newly opened paediatric A&E unit accepted patients from a wide area and not just from Dalverston itself. Built on a separate site to the main hospital, it boasted the most up-to-date facilities available. Everything was geared up for children, from the bright and airy waiting room, which sported comfortable couches rather than the usual hard plastic chairs, to the on-site Radiography unit. X-rays, CT and MRI scans were all carried out in rooms that had been made as child-friendly as possible. Colourful murals adorned the walls and the staff wore brightly coloured polo shirts instead of their usual uniforms. Even the gowns the children were given to wear were printed with cartoon characters and had easy-to-fasten Velcro tabs instead of fiddly ties.

Whilst Mac knew that all these things were incidentals, they helped to put the children at their ease and that, in turn, helped him and the rest of the team do their job. By the time his shift ended, he knew that he was going to enjoy working there. Not only would it allow him to develop his skills in paediatric medicine, but it promised to be a fun place to work too. Several of the nurses were leaving at the same time as him so he held the door open for them, bowing low as they all trooped past.

'After you, ladies,' he said, grinning up at them.

'Thank you, my man,' one of them replied, sticking her nose into the air as she sallied forth.

They all laughed, Mac included, and it was a pleasant change to enjoy a bit of light-hearted banter. He hadn't been overstating how bad things had been on his most recent aid mission. It had been extremely grim at times and it was a relief to feel that he could legitimately enjoy himself, even though he didn't regret going and would do the same thing again if it were necessary. He often thought that he had the best of both worlds: he got to help people who were in dire need of his skills and he also had a job he loved to come back to. There was nothing else he could wish for...except, maybe, someone to share his life.

'Thank you.'

The cool tones brought him up short. Mac straightened abruptly when he recognised Bella's voice, feeling decidedly awkward at being caught on the hop. Although he and Bella had spoken several times during the day, their conversations had been confined to work. He had made sure of it, in fact. Although he had promised himself that he wouldn't say anything to her about Tim, he had realised how hard it was going to be to bite his tongue. Bella had let Tim down. Badly. And it was painful to know that she was capable of such behaviour when he had expected so much more from her.

'You're welcome.' He forced himself to smile even though his insides were churning with all the conflicting emotions. On the one hand he knew it was none of his business, yet on the other it still hurt to know that she had fallen so far short of the picture he had held of her. 'It's been a busy day, hasn't it?' he said, struggling to get his feelings in check. It wouldn't serve any purpose whatsoever to tell her how disappointed he felt, how let down. After all, why should she care how *he* felt when she obviously didn't care about Tim?

'It has. We're seeing more and more children now that word has spread that we're open. Obviously, the other hospitals know we're up and running, but it's the parents bringing in their children that has made the difference.'

She gave a little shrug, immediately drawing his eyes to the slender lines of her body, elegantly encased in an emerald-green coat that he knew without needing to be told was from some exclusive designer's collection. Bella had money—a great deal of money that she had been left by her grandparents—and it showed in the way she dressed, even though she had never flaunted her wealth. It was a tiny point in her favour and Mac found himself clinging to it. Maybe it was silly but he wanted to find something good about her, something to redress the balance a little. His smile was less forced this time.

'It must take the pressure off the other A&E departments if more kids are being treated here. That can only be a good thing.'

'Yes, although so many A&E units have

closed that the ones which are left are still under a great deal of pressure.'

Bella headed towards the car park, making it clear that she didn't expect Mac to accompany her. He hesitated, wondering why he felt so ambivalent all of a sudden. He had been planning an evening doing nothing more taxing than watching television. It was what he needed, some downtime after the hectic couple of months he'd had and yet, surprisingly, he was loath to spend the evening slumped in front of the box. He came to a swift decision even though his brain was telling him that he was making a mistake.

'Do you fancy grabbing a bite to eat?' he said as he caught up with her. He saw the surprise on her face when she glanced round but he ignored it. For some reason he didn't intend to examine too closely, he wanted to spend the evening with her. 'Nothing fancy, just a curry or something.'

'I don't know if it's a good idea.' She stopped and looked him straight in the eyes and he could see the challenge in her gaze. 'It's obvious how you feel, Mac. You blame me for what's happened, don't you?'

'So why don't you set the record straight and tell me your side of the story?'

He shrugged, wishing he felt as indifferent as he was trying to make out. Maybe he was wrong to blame her, but he couldn't help it when he felt so let down. For all these years he had considered her to be the model of perfection and he didn't want to have to change his view of her, especially when he sensed that it could have repercussions. Now that Bella had fallen from her pedestal, she was just a woman like any other. A woman he had always been deeply attracted to.

The thought made his insides churn and he hurried on. 'It seems only fair to me.'

'Sorry, but it isn't going to happen. I have no

intention of trying to justify myself to you or to anyone else.'

She carried on walking, ignoring him as she got into her car. Mac stared after her, wondering why she was being so stubborn. Leaving aside his reasons for wanting to get at the truth, surely it would make sense for her to explain why she had called time on her marriage? Nobody liked being blamed for something they hadn't done and Bella must be no different...

Unless the truth was that she was too embarrassed to admit that she *had* been at fault.

Mac's mouth thinned as he watched her drive away. Bella knew that she had been wrong to abandon Tim when he had needed her so desperately and that was why she couldn't face the thought of talking about it. Although his opinion of her had already dropped way down the scale, it slid even further. Bella was a long way from being perfect, it seemed.

* * *

Bella spent a miserable evening. Not even the latest bestseller could take her mind off what had happened. Should she have done as Mac had suggested and told him her version—the *real* version—about what had gone on?

She kept mulling it over, wishing that she had and then just as quickly dismissing the idea. Once she set off down that route there would be no turning back; she would have to wait and see if Mac believed her. The thought that he might think she was lying was more than she could bear. It would be better not to say anything rather than have to endure his contempt.

She was due in to work at lunchtime the following day. By the time she arrived, there was quite a long queue of patients waiting to be seen. Janet waved as she crossed Reception and Bella waved back although she didn't stop. There was a child screaming and it seemed propitious to go and check what was happening before the other children started to get upset. The noise was coming from the treatment room so she went straight there, frowning when she opened the door and was assailed by the shrill screams of an angry toddler.

'What's going on?' she asked, dropping her coat onto a chair.

'Alfie fell off his scooter and cut his knee,' Laura Watson, one of their most experienced nurses, told her. She rolled her eyes. 'Unfortunately, he won't let me look at it 'cos it's sore.'

'I see.' Bella crouched down in front of the little boy. He was clinging to an older woman who she guessed was his grandmother. 'That's an awful lot of noise, Alfie. You're going to scare Robbie if you scream like that.'

The little boy stopped screaming and peeped at her through his fingers, distracted by the mention of the unknown Robbie. Bella smiled at him. 'That's better. Have you met Robbie yet? He's rather shy and only comes out of his cupboard when he thinks nobody is looking. I'll go and see if I can find him.'

Standing up, she crossed the room and opened one of the cupboards that held their supplies. Robbie, the toy rabbit, was sitting on a shelf so she lifted him down and carried him back to the little boy.

'Here he is. He must like you, Alfie, because he came straight out of his cupboard and didn't try to hide.' She handed the toy to the child then glanced at the older woman. 'If you could pop him on the bed then I can take a look at his knee,' she said sotto voce.

The woman quickly complied, sighing with relief when Alfie carried on playing with the toy. 'Thank heavens for that! I thought he would never stop screaming.' She smiled at Bella. 'You must have children, my dear. It's obvious that you know just how to distract them.'

'Sadly, no, I don't.'

Bella smiled, trying to ignore the pang of regret that pierced her heart. Having a family had always been her dearest wish, something she had assumed would happen once she had got married, but Tim had never been keen on the idea. Whenever she had broached the subject, he had brushed it aside, claiming that he had no intention of being tied down by a baby at that stage in his life. It was only after she had told him that she wanted a divorce that he had tried to persuade her to stay with promises of them starting a family, but she had refused. The last thing she'd wanted was to have a child to hold their marriage together, a sticking-plaster baby.

'Then you should.' Alfie's grandmother laughed ruefully as she ruffled her grandson's hair. 'Oh, they're hard work, but having children is one of life's blessings. And there's no doubt that you'd make a wonderful mother!'

* * *

Mac paused outside the treatment room. The door was ajar and he had heard every word. He frowned as he recalled the regret in Bella's voice when she had explained that she didn't have any children. Quite frankly, he couldn't understand it. According to Tim, Bella had refused his pleas to start a family, claiming that her career came first and that having children was way down her list of priorities, but it hadn't sounded like that, had it? It made him wonder all of a sudden if Tim had been telling him the truth.

It was the first time that Mac had considered the idea that his friend might not have been totally honest and it troubled him. He had accepted what Tim had said without question but had he been right to do so? What if Tim had tried to cast himself in a more favourable light by laying the blame on Bella? What if it hadn't been all her fault that the marriage had failed? What if Tim had been more than partly to blame?

After all, it couldn't have been easy for her to cope with Tim's dependence on those pain-killers. Mac had worked in a rehab unit and he knew from experience how unreasonable people could be when they were in the throes of an addiction. Bella must have been through the mill—struggling to help Tim conquer his addiction, struggling to support him even when his behaviour probably hadn't been as good as it should have been. As he made his way to the cubicles, Mac realised that he needed to get to the bottom of what had gone on. Although Tim was his oldest friend, he owed it to Bella to ascertain the true facts. The thought that he might have misjudged her didn't sit easily with him, quite frankly.

Mac didn't get a chance to speak to Bella until it was almost time for him to go off duty. He was on his way to the office when he saw her coming along the corridor. She gave him a cool smile as she went to walk past, but there was no way that he was prepared to leave matters the way they were. It was too important that they got this sorted out, even though he wasn't sure why it seemed so urgent.

'Have you got a second?' he asked, putting out his hand. His fingers brushed against her arm and he felt a flash of something akin to an electric current shoot through him. It was all he could do to maintain an outward show of composure when it felt as though his pulse was fizzing from the charge. 'There's something I need to ask you.'

'I'm just on my way to phone the lab about some results I need,' she said quietly. However, he heard the tremor in her voice and realised that she had felt it too, felt that surge of electricity that had passed between them.

'Oh, right. Well, I won't hold you up. Maybe we can meet later? You're due a break soon, aren't you? How about coffee in the canteen?' he suggested, struggling to get a grip. What on earth was going on? This was Bella, Tim's wife—OK, technically, she was Tim's *ex-wife*—but it still didn't seem right that he should be acting this way, yet he couldn't seem to stop it.

'Why? I don't mean to be rude, Mac, but why do you want us to have coffee?'

She stared back at him, her green eyes searching his face in a way that made him feel more than a little uncomfortable. If he came straight out and admitted that he wanted to check if she was solely to blame for the demise of her marriage then it would hardly endear him to her, would it? He came to a swift decision.

'Because we need to clear the air.' He shrugged, opting for a half-truth rather than the full monty. 'I get the impression that working with me is a strain for you, Bella, and it's not what I want. It's not what you want either, I expect.'

'You're imagining it. I don't have a problem about working with you.' She gave him a chilly smile. 'Now, if you'll excuse me…'

She walked away, leaving him wishing that he hadn't said anything. After all, he hadn't achieved anything, probably made things even more awkward, in fact.

Mac sighed as he made his way to the office. That would teach him to poke his nose into matters that didn't concern him. What had gone on between Tim and Bella was their business and he would be well advised to leave alone.

Bella worked straight through without even stopping for a break. Although they were busy, she could have taken a few minutes off if she'd wanted to, but she didn't. Mac's request to talk to her had unsettled her and she preferred to keep her mind on her patients rather than worry about it. She dealt with her final patient, a ten-year-old boy who had fallen off his bike and broken his arm. Once the X-rays had confirmed her diagnosis, she sent him to the plaster room and cleared up. Helen Robertson, one of the new F1s on the unit, grinned when Bella made her way to the nurses' station to sign out.

'Off home to put your feet up, are you? Or are you planning a wild night out?'

'No chance. It's straight home, supper and bed for me,' Bella replied with a laugh. 'My days of tripping the light fantastic are well and truly over!'

'Oh, listen to her. You'd think she was in her dotage, wouldn't you?' Helen looked past Bella and raised her brows. 'Maybe you can convince her that she can forgo the carpet slippers for a while longer!'

Bella glanced round to see who Helen was

talking to and felt her heart lurch when she saw Mac standing behind her. She knew that he was supposed to have gone off duty several hours before and couldn't understand what he was doing there... Unless he had stayed behind to talk to her? The thought filled her with dread. She didn't want to talk to him about anything, neither her marriage nor what Tim had and hadn't done. If she told Mac then she would have to face the possibility that he might not believe her and she couldn't bear that, couldn't stand to know that he thought she was lying.

She hurriedly signed her name in the register, adding the time of her departure. Mac was still talking to Helen, laughing at something the young doctor had said, so Bella headed for the door. It hummed open and she was outside, walking as fast as she could towards the car park. She could hear footsteps behind her and knew that Mac was following her but she didn't slow down. He had no business harassing her this way! She had made it perfectly clear that she didn't intend to discuss her marriage with him and he should accept that. All of a sudden anger got the better of her and she swung round.

'Please stop! I don't want to talk to you, so leave me alone.'

'Why? What are you so scared about?' He shrugged. 'If I were in your shoes, I'd want to tell my side of the story, unless I had something to hide. Do you, Bella?'

'No.' She gave a bitter little laugh, unable to hide how hurt she felt at the suggestion. 'I have nothing to hide but Tim's told you what happened, and you obviously believe him, so what more is there to say? Why should I try to justify myself to you?'

'Because I thought we were friends.' He held out his hands, palms up, in a gesture of supplication that she found incredibly moving for some reason. 'I can tell that you're hurting and if there's anything I can do to make it easier for you then that's all I want.'

He paused. Bella had a feeling that he wasn't sure if he should say what was on his mind and she bit her lip because she wasn't sure if she wanted to hear it either. She steeled herself when he continued.

'I guess what I'm trying to say is that I care about you, Bella. It's as simple as that.'

CHAPTER THREE

MAC HELD HIS BREATH, hoping against hope that Bella would believe him. It was the truth, after all—he *did* care. He cared that she was hurting, cared that she had behaved so out of character. The Bella he knew would *never* have broken her marriage vows unless there had been a very good reason to do so.

'Maybe you mean what you say, Mac, but it makes no difference.' Bella's icy tones sliced through the thoughts whizzing around his head and he flinched.

'I do mean it,' he said shortly, annoyed with himself. What possible reason could there be to excuse the way she had treated Tim? Tim had needed her, desperately, and she had failed him. There was no excuse whatsoever for that kind of behaviour, surely? And yet the niggling little doubt refused to go away.

'Fine.'

She inclined her head but Mac could tell that she didn't believe him and it stung to know that she doubted his word. Couldn't she see that he was telling her the truth? Didn't she know that he wouldn't lie about something so important? It was on the tip of his tongue to remonstrate with her when it struck him that he was doing the very same thing. He was doubting *her*, blaming *her* for the demise of her marriage. What right did he have to take her to task when he was equally guilty?

The thought kept him silent and she obviously took it as a sign that he had given up. She went to her car, zapping the locks and getting in. Mac stayed where he was until the sound of the engine roused him. He had no idea what he was going to do but he had to do something.

Maybe Bella was at fault, but he couldn't just ignore the pain he had seen in her eyes. Flinging open the passenger door, he climbed into her car, holding up his hand when she rounded on him.

'I know what you're going to say, Bella. You don't want to talk about your marriage. I also know that I'm probably poking my nose in where it's not wanted...'

'You are,' she snapped, glaring at him.

'OK. Fair enough. And I'm sorry. But, leaving all that aside, I meant what I said. I really do care that you're upset.' He reached over and squeezed her hand, hurriedly releasing it when he felt the now familiar surge of electricity scorch along his nerves. He didn't want to scare her, certainly didn't want her to think that he was trying to take advantage of her vulnerability by making a play for her!

Heat rose under his skin, a hot tide of embarrassment that was so unfamiliar that it would have brought him to his knees if he hadn't been sitting down. Making a play for Bella had never been on the cards. From the moment they had met, Mac had known that she was beyond his reach and he had been perfectly happy with that state of affairs too. Although he had earned himself a bit of a reputation at university by dating a lot of women, he'd had no intention of settling down. He had been determined not to get involved with anyone, although he had been genuinely pleased when Bella and Tim had started seeing one another. They had been so well suited, their backgrounds so perfectly in tune that he couldn't have found a better match for either of them.

It had been the same when they had announced their engagement some months later; he had been truly thrilled for them both and absolutely delighted when Tim had asked him to be his best man. It was only at the wedding that he had started to feel a little bit odd. Listening to Bella swearing to love, honour and care for Tim for the rest of her days had, surprisingly, made Mac feel as though he was about to lose something unutterably precious...

He drove the thought from his head. It was too late for it now; far too late to wish that he had said something, done something, stopped the wedding. How could he have jumped up in the middle of the ceremony and declared that he didn't want Bella to marry Tim because he wanted her for *himself*? No, he had done the right thing—sat there and played his part to the best of his ability. And if there'd been an ache in his heart, well, he had accepted that he would have to learn to live with it.

That was why he had decided to sign on with Worlds Together, a leading overseas aid agency, after the wedding. He had been on over half a dozen missions to date and although he knew that he had helped a lot of people during that time, he had gained a lot too. He'd had three years to rationalise his feelings, three years to make sure they were safely under wraps. Why, if anyone had asked him a couple of weeks ago how he felt then he would have confidently told them that he was back on track. But not now. Not now that Bella was no longer Tim's wife. Not now that she was available.

Mac swallowed his groan. Maybe he did want to help Bella but it could turn out that he was creating a lot of problems for himself by doing so.

Bella had no idea what was going on but the tension in the car was making her feel sick. She licked her parched lips, trying to think of something to say, but what exactly? If she ordered Mac to get out of the car, would he do so? Or would he ignore her and stay where he was? It was the not knowing that was the scariest thing of all because it denoted a massive shift in his attitude.

Mac's behaviour towards her had always been impeccable in the past. He had treated her with an old-fashioned courtesy that she had found strangely endearing. Few men in the circles she had frequented had been so polite. The old 'Hooray Henry' syndrome had been very much alive, so that Mac's thoughtfulness and maturity had set him apart. That was why she had enjoyed spending time with him, she realised in surprise. He hadn't needed to shout or tell risqué stories to make himself stand out. Whenever Mac was around, people always knew he was there.

The thought stunned her. She had never realised before just how much Mac had impressed her. He had been an unknown quantity in so many ways, his background so different from hers that she had been afraid of saying something stupid that would betray her ignorance. Now, after working in the NHS for the past ten years, she had a much better idea of the world. She had treated many people from backgrounds similar to Mac's and understood the hardships they faced. That Mac must have had to overcome all sorts of obstacles to qualify as a doctor merely highlighted his strength of character, his determination, his commitment. Few men could have taken on such a challenge and won.

Bella's head whirled as thoughts that she had never entertained before rushed through it. Added to the strain she'd been under since the breakdown of her marriage, it made her feel very shaky. Leaning forward, she rested her throbbing forehead on the steering wheel.

'Are you all right? Bella, what's wrong? Answer me!'

The concern in Mac's voice brought a rush of tears to her eyes. Although her parents had expressed polite sympathy when she had told them about the divorce, they hadn't really cared about the effect it had had on her. They were too wrapped up in their own lives to put her first. As Mac had just done.

'It's just all too much,' she whispered, unable to lie.

'No wonder!' Anger laced his deep voice as he got out of the car. He strode round to her side and flung open the door. 'When I think what you must have been through recently—' He broke off as he lifted her out of the car. Bella got the impression that he didn't trust himself to say anything more as he carried her round to the passenger's side. He gently deposited her on the seat and snapped the seat belt into place then looked at her. 'Right, where to? You can go straight home or you can come back to my place. You decide.'

Bella bit her lip as she weighed up her choices, even though by rights she knew that she should tell him to take her home. She didn't want to talk to him, especially not tonight when she felt so raw, so emotional, so very vulnerable.

'Come on, Bella. Just choose where you want to go and I'll take you there.' His tone was so gentle, so persuasive, and Bella wanted to be persuaded so much...

'Yours.'

Mac nodded as he closed the door. Walking round to the driver's side, he got in and backed out of the parking space. He didn't say a word as he drove out of the hospital gates. Bella had no idea where he lived and quite frankly didn't care. Wherever it was, it had to be better than the soulless apartment she was renting. They drove for about fifteen minutes, the roads becoming increasingly narrow as they headed away from the town centre. Bella had done very little exploring since she had moved to Dalverston and had no idea where they were going until she saw the pale glint of water in the distance and realised they were heading towards the river. Mac slowed and turned down a narrow lane, drawing up on the grass verge.

'We have to walk from here,' he told her. 'It's not far, just five minutes or so, but we can't take the car any further.'

Bella nodded as she unfastened her seat belt. She slid to the ground, breathing in the musky scent of damp vegetation. She could hear the river now, the softly sibilant whisper of the water providing a backdrop to the sound of the birds performing their evening chorus. It was so peaceful that she sighed.

'It's wonderful not to hear any traffic.'

'One of the big advantages of living out in the sticks,' Mac replied with a smile that made her breath catch.

He turned and led the way along the path, leaving her to follow, which she did once she had got her breath back. It was the way he had smiled at her that had done the damage— smiled at her the way Mac had used to do. Did it mean that he had forgiven her for her apparent misdemeanours? She doubted it, yet all of a sudden she felt better than she had done in ages. The world didn't seem quite so grim now that Mac had smiled at her. How crazy was that?

Mac paused when they reached the riverbank. It was almost nine p.m. and the light was fading fast. In another month, there would still be enough daylight to light their way along the towpath but he was afraid that Bella would trip up in the dark. Holding out his hand, he smiled at her, determined to keep a rein on his emotions this time. He was offering to hold her hand for safety's sake and not for his own nefarious reasons!

'You'd better hold on to me. The path's a bit slippery after all the rain we've had recently. I don't want you ending up taking a dip.'

There was a moment when he sensed her

hesitate before she slipped her hand into his. Mac sucked in his breath when he felt his libido immediately stir to life. OK, so, admittedly, he hadn't made love to a woman in a very long time, but that had been his choice, hadn't it? He had grown tired of dating for dating's sake, had become weary of sex that hadn't really meant anything. It had seemed better to step out of the game rather than continue the way he had been doing. However, it was completely out of order for him to start lusting after Bella. She'd been through enough without him making her life even more complicated.

Mac gave himself a stern talking-to as he led her along the towpath and, thankfully, it seemed to work. There were several boats tied up along the riverbank and he guided her around their mooring lines. They came to the last boat in the row and he stopped, suddenly feeling on edge as he wondered what she would make of his home. Although he loved the old boat—loved everything about it, from the tranquillity of its mooring to the fact that it was the first home he had owned—Bella had been brought up to expect so much more. He couldn't help feeling a little bit…well, *nervous* about what she would make of it.

'This is it,' he announced, wincing when he heard the false note of bonhomie in his voice. It wasn't like him to put up a front and he hated the fact that he'd felt it necessary. If Bella didn't like his home—so what? It wouldn't make a scrap of difference to him… Would it?

'You live on a boat!'

The surprise in her voice made his teeth snap together as he forced down the urge to start apologising.

'Yep. I bought it when I moved here. I couldn't afford a house so I opted for this instead. It's the perfect base when I'm in the UK. Come on. I'll show you round.'

He helped her on board and unlocked the cabin door, turning on the oil lamp so that she could see where she was going. 'The steps are quite steep,' he warned her. 'So take your time.'

Bella nodded as she cautiously stepped down into the cabin. Mac followed her, turning on more lamps as he went so that the cabin was suddenly bathed in light. Bella stopped and looked around, her face looking even more beautiful in the lamplight. And Mac's libido wriggled that little bit further out of its box.

'It's beautiful. So warm and welcoming... Oh, I do envy you living here, Mac. It must be marvellous!'

There was no doubt that she was telling him the truth and Mac's nerves evaporated in a rush of pleasure. He had no idea why it meant so much to hear her praise his home but it did. He laughed out loud.

'I was worried in case you hated it,' he confessed as his confidence came surging back. 'After all, it is *rather* different from what you're accustomed to.'

'And that's why I love it so much,' she said simply. 'You can keep all your architectural gems as far as I'm concerned. I much prefer somewhere like this—a real home.'

She sat down on the old couch that he had spent so many hours reupholstering and smiled up at him. Mac felt himself melt as relief washed over him. Bella liked his home—she *genuinely* liked it! He wanted to leap up and punch the air in triumph even though he knew how stupid it was.

'Thank you, although you'd better not be too lavish with the compliments or I'll get a swelled head,' he said, trying to joke his way through such a truly amazing moment. 'Not a good idea in a place as small as this!'

'Not small—compact. Or maybe that should be bijou if you prefer estate agent speak.'

Her smile was gentle, making him wonder if she had guessed how nervous he'd felt, but how could she? Bella had no idea that he had always felt at a disadvantage around her in the past, thanks to his background. He had gone to great lengths to hide his feelings and had thought that he had succeeded too. Thankfully, he no longer felt that way. The passage of time had given him the confidence to accept himself for who he was, which was why it was all the more surprising that he had been worried about her reaction.

'Hmm, I'm not sure if most estate agents would class it as that,' he replied lightly, not wanting her to guess how disturbed he felt. He hadn't realised that she understood him so well, hadn't thought that she even *cared* enough to try. And that thought was the last one he needed when he and his libido were having such a hard time sorting themselves out.

'Right. I'll make us some coffee.'

He hurriedly set about filling the kettle. Opening a cupboard, he took out a couple of mugs and placed them on the worktop. There was fresh milk in the tiny fridge and sugar in the jar so he fetched them as well. By the time he had done all that, he was feeling far more in control. Maybe it had come as a surprise to discover that Bella knew him rather better than he had thought she did, but he wasn't going to allow it to throw him off course. Maybe he *did* want to hold her, kiss her, do all sorts of things to her he had never even contemplated before, but he wasn't going to forfeit their friendship for a night of rampant sex. Bella was too important to him; he cared too much about her. And not even what Tim had told him could change that.

It was a moment of revelation, a light-bulb moment that suddenly made everything so much clearer. He may have accepted what Tim had told him. He may even have been hurt and angry about what Bella had done, but he still cared about her. And he always would.

'Thank you.' Bella accepted the cup of coffee. It was too hot to drink and she set it down on the table in front of the couch.

Everything was scaled down to fit, yet, surprisingly, it didn't feel cramped. She found herself comparing it to the vast amount of space in her rented apartment and realised that she much preferred it here. In fact, she had never felt so at ease in any of her previous homes, not even the house she and Tim had started their married life in.

Tim's parents had insisted on buying the elegant Georgian town house for them as a wedding present and her parents, not to be outdone, had insisted on furnishing it. However, the designer-styled rooms with their expensive furniture and luxurious fabrics couldn't hold a candle to this place, she decided. The house had been more an expression of wealth than a real home and it was a relief not to have to live there any longer.

The thought immediately made her feel guilty. It reminded her of how relieved she'd been when she had finally plucked up the courage to leave. It had taken her months of soul-searching before she had reached her decision and it still hurt to know that she had broken her marriage vows, even though she'd had no choice. Tim's behaviour had become increasingly erratic by that point; he had become a danger to his patients as well as to himself. Leaving him had been the only thing she could think of to shock him into seeking help and it had worked too. But did Mac understand that? Did he understand just how hard it had been for her to break her vows? All of a sudden Bella knew that she needed to find out.

'It wasn't an easy decision to leave Tim,' she said quietly. Out of the corner of her eye, she saw Mac stiffen and experienced a momentary qualm. She had sworn that she wouldn't try to justify her actions, but she needed to make Mac understand how impossible the situation had been. 'I agonised over it for months but in the end I realised that I didn't have a choice. It was the only thing I could think of that might bring him to his senses.'

'Wouldn't it have been better if you'd stayed and encouraged him to get help?' Mac suggested and she flinched when she heard the cynicism in his voice.

'I tried that, but Tim refused to listen to anything I said. He insisted that he didn't have a problem and that I was making a fuss about nothing.' She shrugged, recalling the vicious arguments they'd had. The drugs had changed Tim from the man she had married into someone she had barely recognised. 'He couldn't see that he was addicted to the painkillers and needed help.'

'So you upped and left him?'

Mac regarded her from beneath lowered lids. It was hard to tell what he was thinking, although she could guess. Mac believed that she should have stayed with Tim no matter what, but he hadn't been there, had he? He hadn't witnessed the rows, the lies, the empty, meaningless promises to stop taking the drugs.

'Yes. I hoped that it would shock him into admitting that he had a problem and it worked too. He went into rehab a couple of weeks later.'

'I see. So why didn't you go back once he was clean?' Mac's brows rose. 'Tim told me that he begged you to go back to him but you refused. If you loved him then surely that would have been the right thing to do?'

'It wasn't that simple,' Bella said quietly. She stared down at her hands, wondering if she should tell him about Tim's affair. Would she have gone back if she hadn't found out about it or had it been the excuse she had needed? Her feelings for Tim had reached rock-bottom by then; the thought of trying to make their marriage work had filled her with dread. The truth of the matter was that she had no longer loved him, always assuming that she had loved him in the first place, which she now doubted.

'No? It seems pretty straightforward to me.' Mac's tone was harsh. 'What about all those promises you made when you got married? Were they just so many empty words at the end of the day?'

'Of course not!' Bella said angrily, hating the fact he seemed determined to blame her for everything. 'I meant every word I said, but it needs two people to uphold a promise, although Tim obviously didn't see it that way.'

'What do you mean?' Mac shot back. 'It was you who left him.'

'Forget it. It doesn't matter.'

Bella picked up her coffee mug, feeling infinitely weary. No matter what she said, Mac would continue to blame her. Even if she told him about Tim's affair, there was no way of knowing if he would believe her. The thought that he might think she was lying about that to save face was more than she could bear. It would be better to say nothing than take that risk.

They finished their coffee in silence. Bella put her mug on the table and rose to her feet. It was gone ten p.m. and time she went home, even though the prospect of going back to the apartment wasn't appealing. 'I'd better go. Thank you for the coffee and everything.'

'Do you know how to get back?' Mac asked gruffly.

'I'll use the satnav.' She bent and picked up her bag, swaying a little as exhaustion suddenly caught up with her. It had been a long day and add to that the ongoing guilt she felt about the divorce and it was little wonder that she felt so drained.

'Sit down.' Mac eased her back down onto the couch. Taking the bag off her, he placed it on the table then crouched down in front of her. 'There's no way that you can drive yourself home in this state. You'll have to stay here tonight.'

'Oh, but I couldn't possibly,' Bella began but he ignored her. Standing up, he crossed the cabin and opened a door at the far end to reveal a tiny bedroom complete with double bed.

'You can sleep in here,' he informed her brusquely. Picking up one of the oil lamps, he placed it on the shelf next to the bed, turning down the wick so that the room was bathed in a soft golden glow. 'The sheets are clean and you should be comfortable enough. Bathroom's through there,' he continued, pointing to a door leading off from the bedroom. 'It's only basic but there's everything you'll need.'

'But where are you going to sleep?' Bella protested, more tempted than she cared to admit. Maybe it was foolish but the thought of staying on the boat was the most wonderful thing she could think of. She felt safe here— safe, secure, protected: all the things she hadn't felt in ages.

'The couch pulls out into a bed so don't worry about me,' Mac told her. Opening a cupboard, he took out a T-shirt and tossed it onto the bed. 'You can use this to sleep in. I haven't anything else, I'm afraid.'

'It's fine. Thank you,' Bella said softly.

She sank down onto the bed after Mac left, feeling the last vestige of strength drain from her limbs. Picking up the T-shirt, she held it to her cheek, savouring the softness of the cotton against her skin. Tears filled her eyes again and she blinked them away but more kept on coming, pouring down her face in a scalding-hot tide. She hadn't cried before, not even when Tim had said all those awful things to her after she had told him that she wanted a divorce. Now Mac's kindness had unleashed all the feelings she had held in check and they came spilling out, all the hurt and the pain, the guilt and the relief, every single thing, including how she felt about Mac himself.

Bella took a deep breath. She didn't want to think about Mac and how confused he made her feel. It had always been the same and yet she couldn't understand why he made her feel so mixed up. Normally she had no difficulty making up her mind. Every decision she had ever made had been carefully considered, rationalised, even when she had agreed to marry Tim.

Marrying Tim had seemed like the right thing to do. He had come from a similar background to hers, had held the same values as well as the same expectations. To her mind, their marriage was bound to be a success; however, with the benefit of hindsight, she could see that it hadn't been enough. It had needed more than the fact that they had been compatible on paper—her feelings for Tim had needed to be much stronger, especially after he had become addicted to those drugs. She had failed Tim because she hadn't cared enough, because she wasn't sure if she was *capable* of feeling that deeply about anyone.

Lying down on the bed, Bella clutched the T-shirt to her as sorrow overwhelmed her. She had spent so many years ignoring her emotions that she had lost touch with them. No wonder she couldn't understand how she felt about Mac.

CHAPTER FOUR

THE GENTLE MOTION of the boat woke Mac from a restless sleep. It had been the early hours of the morning before he had finally dozed off, his mind too busy to allow him to rest. Last night had been unsettling for so many reasons, the main one being that Bella had slept right here on the boat. Several times he had heard her crying and he'd had a devil of a job to stop himself going to her. However, the thought of what might happen if he did had helped him control the urge. It would have been far too easy to allow the need to comfort her to turn into something more.

His body responded with predictable enthusiasm to that thought and he groaned. He had to stop this! Maybe it was time he thought about breaking his self-imposed vow of celibacy. So what if sex had become merely a physical release, like an itch that needed scratching? Surely it would be better to deal with the itch than allow it to turn into a major problem.

Rolling out of bed, he filled the kettle and set it to boil then opened the hatch to let some fresh air into the cabin. It had been raining through the night and he grimaced as raindrops splashed onto his head and shoulders. Picking up a tea towel, he dried his face then looked round when he heard the bedroom door open, his heart lurching when he saw Bella standing in the doorway. She was wearing the T-shirt he had lent her and although it came midway down her thighs there was still an awful lot of her shapely legs on view. His gaze ran over her, greedily drinking in every detail. Although his T-shirt was huge on her, somehow the washed thin cotton managed to cling to her body, outlining the curve of her hips, the hand-span narrowness of her waist, the swell of her breasts...

Mac sucked in a great lungful of air when he saw her nipples suddenly pucker beneath the cotton. Rationally, he knew that it was no more than a physical response to the chilly air flowing through the cabin, but after the night he'd had, thinking rationally wasn't easy. His wayward thoughts flew off at a tangent as he found himself imagining how it would feel to watch her nipples harden as he caressed her...

He groaned out loud, hurriedly turning it into a cough when he saw her look at him in alarm. 'Hmm, a bit of a frog in the throat this morning,' he muttered, reaching for the coffee.

'It is a bit chilly in here,' she replied, hugging her arms around herself, and Mac saw the exact second when she realised what was happening. Colour rushed up her face as she hurried back into the bedroom. Picking up her sweater from the end of the bed, she dragged it over her head. 'That's better,' she said brightly as she turned round.

Mac wanted to disagree. He wanted to do it so badly that the words got all clumped up in his throat and almost choked him. He had to content himself with nodding, which was probably the safest response anyway.

'Anything I can do? Make the coffee? Or how about some toast—I could make that, if you like?'

Bella hovered uncertainly in the doorway and Mac's feelings underwent yet another rapid change. Tenderness swamped him as he pointed to the bread bin. Bella's composure was legendary. Even when they'd been students, she had always appeared to be totally in control. He couldn't remember her looking so out of her depth before, so that all he wanted to do was to put her at ease.

'Seeing as you've volunteered, you can be on

toast duty. There's no toaster, I'm afraid. You have to do it the old-fashioned way under the grill.' He lit the grill for her. 'Butter's in the fridge and there's marmalade in that cupboard over there.' He pointed everything out then headed to the bedroom. 'I'll have a shower while you're doing that if it's OK with you?'

'Of course.'

Bella nodded as she took a loaf out of the bread bin. Picking up the bread knife, she started to cut it into slices, the tip of her pink tongue poking out between her lips. Mac turned away, not proof against any more temptations so early in the day. He didn't want to think about her tongue and how it would feel stroking his...

There was plenty of hot water for a shower but he turned the dial to cold instead. Stepping under the icy spray, he shivered violently. If there was one thing he loathed more than anything else it was a cold shower but he didn't deserve a hot one, not after the way he'd been behaving.

Lusting after Bella simply wasn't on! Quite apart from the fact that it would ruin whatever friendship they had, he couldn't do it to Tim. Tim may have kicked his drug habit but, like any addict, he was very vulnerable. Mac couldn't bear to imagine the harm it could cause if he and Bella had an affair, not that it was on the cards, of course. However, the fact that he was even *thinking* about Bella in such terms was a warning in itself. Now that she had forfeited her married status, it didn't mean that he was free to make a play for her. No, to all intents and purposes nothing had changed. It was still Bella and Tim.

Bella had their breakfast ready by the time Mac reappeared. He was wearing a pair of navy chinos with a blue-and-white striped shirt, and it was a relief to see him safely cov-

ered up. Maybe he had been decent enough before but the T-shirt and shorts he had worn to
sleep in hadn't left very much to the imagina-
tion. To her mind, there'd been a rather disturbing amount of leanly muscular body on show.

Heat flowed under her skin as she hurriedly
placed the toast on the table. She added the
coffee pot along with the milk jug and sugar
bowl, determined not to allow her mind to get
hijacked by any more such foolish ideas. She
had seen men wearing a lot less than Mac had
worn that morning in the course of her work
so it was stupid to start acting like some sort
of...*inexperienced virgin*!

'I could grow used to this.' Mac grinned as
he sat down and reached for the coffee pot. He
filled both of the mugs, adding milk and several spoons of sugar to his. 'It's a real treat to
have my breakfast made for me.'

'It's the least I can do,' Bella murmured, sitting down opposite him. Her knees bumped

against his and she hastily drew her legs back out of the way, steadfastly ignoring the odd tingling sensation that seemed to be spreading from the point where their knees had touched.

She was bound to feel *aware* of him, she reasoned, adding a dash of milk to her coffee. After all, it wasn't as though she had made a habit of spending the night with a man, was it? She had never had an affair, had never even indulged in any one-night stands like so many of her contemporaries at university had done. She had only ever slept with Tim, in fact, so spending the night with Mac was a whole new experience for her.

The thought unsettled her even more. It seemed to imply that she'd had an ulterior motive for spending the night on the boat. It wasn't true, of course; it had been necessity that had forced her to stay, the need to rest and recoup her strength. The past year had been extremely hard. Between the stress of the divorce and the move to Dalverston, it was little wonder that it had felt as though she had reached rock-bottom last night. However, she felt much better this morning, less anxious and more like her old self. Spending the night here with Mac had worked wonders and it was just a shame that she couldn't do it again.

Bella bit into her toast, more surprised by that thought than she could say. Bearing in mind how confused Mac made her feel, she should be trying to avoid him, surely? And yet there was no denying that if he had offered to let her stay again tonight *and* the night after that, she would have accepted with alacrity. Being with Mac might be unsettling but in a good way.

They finished their breakfast, making desultory conversation as they ate. Mac sighed as he drained the last dregs of coffee from his mug. 'I'd better get a move on or I'll be late. Are you working today?'

'No.' Bella picked up her mug and plate. She carried them to the tiny sink and pumped water into the bowl. 'I'm working over the weekend so I've got today and tomorrow off.'

'Lucky you.' Mac picked up his dishes and brought them over to the sink. He checked his watch and grimaced. 'I really will have to fly. Fingers crossed that they haven't changed the times of the buses, otherwise I am going to be seriously late.'

'Bus? Why do you need to take the bus?' Bella queried, rinsing their mugs and setting them to drain.

'I left my motorbike at the hospital last night.'

Bella sighed. 'Because you drove me back here? Of course. Sorry.'

'It doesn't matter.' He reached for his jacket, patting the pockets to check that he had everything. 'Look, I'm sorry but I'm going to have to cut and run…'

'Here. Take my car.' Bella picked up her car

keys. She shook her head when he started to protest. 'I insist. It's my fault that you left your motorbike at the hospital so it's the least I can do.'

'But what about you?' he demanded, his dark brows drawing together. 'How are you going to get home?'

'Don't worry about me. I'll call a taxi.' Bella pressed the keys into his hand. 'Go on, off you go or you'll be late.'

'Yes, ma'am.' Mac grinned at her. 'Has anyone told you how bossy you are?'

'Not lately,' Bella retorted. She followed him up to the deck, pausing when he stopped. His blue eyes were very dark as they met hers.

'Sure you'll be OK? I feel as though I'm abandoning you.'

'Don't be silly,' she said briskly, although she was deeply touched by the sentiment. It had been a long time since anyone had worried about her this way. 'I'll be perfectly fine.

I'll tidy up then phone for a cab… Oh, wait, what's the address? I've no idea where we are.'

'Too-Good Lane.' Mac dug into his pockets and pulled out a crumpled supermarket receipt. He jotted down a number on the back and handed it to her. 'Phone Dennis and ask him to come for you. He's a nice chap and very reliable. You'll be safe with him.'

'Oh, right. Thank you.' Bella went to slip the paper into her pocket before she remembered that she didn't have any pockets. She took a hasty step back when she spotted a jogger running along the towpath, suddenly conscious of her state of undress. She could just imagine what people would think if they saw her standing here wearing one of Mac's T-shirts. They would assume that she and Mac had spent the night together and, although they had, they hadn't *slept* together! Heat flowed under her skin as the thought triggered a whole raft of images: Mac's eyes, so deep and dark as he stared down at her; the feel of his hands as he stroked her body from throat to thigh…

A shudder passed through her and she turned away, terrified that she would give herself away. She heard Mac call a cheery goodbye as he leapt off the boat, even managed to respond, but everything seemed to be happening at one step removed. All she could think about were Mac's hands stroking and caressing her.

Bella hurried back inside the cabin and stood there with her arms hugged tightly around herself. She had never felt this way before, never experienced this overwhelming surge of desire. Although she had enjoyed making love with Tim in the beginning, she had never yearned for his touch. However, with a sudden rush of insight she realised that if Mac made love to her it would be very different. She wouldn't be able to remain detached then—she wouldn't want to. If Mac made love to her, she would be unable to hold anything back, not even a tiny scrap of herself. Mac would unleash her passion, awaken her desire and, once that happened, it would be impossible to go back.

She shuddered. She would be changed for ever, a completely different person, a woman who not only felt but *needed* to feel too. She wasn't sure if she could cope with that.

Mac was thrown in at the deep end as soon as he arrived at work. There'd been an accident on the by-pass involving a lorry and a coach ferrying children to the local high school. Thirty-three casualties were brought through their doors and each one needed to be assessed and treated. Fortunately, Trish Baxter, one of their most experienced staff nurses, was on duty and she performed triage. The less seriously injured children—those with only minor cuts and bruises—were told to wait while the rest were farmed out between cubicles, treatment rooms and Resus. Fortunately, there were just two children badly injured enough to require the facilities of resuscitation and Mac dealt with them. Twelve-year-old twins, Emily and Ethan Harris, had been sitting together at the exact spot where the truck had hit the coach.

'Hi, I'm Mac and I'm a doctor,' Mac explained as the paramedics rolled the youngsters in on their respective trolleys. He listened attentively while the crew outlined the children's status. Emily had injuries to her right arm and was in a great deal of pain, while her brother was having difficulty breathing. Ethan had been thrown into the aisle by the force of the impact and trapped under the seat, which had come away from its housing. It was more than likely that he had fractured ribs which could be compromising his breathing if they had pierced the pleura—the two layers of membrane that covered the lungs and the chest wall. If blood had entered the pleura cavity it would compress the lungs and cause a partial collapse. Mac knew that the boy required urgent treatment and turned to Helen Robertson, the F1 student, who was working with him.

'You take the girl. She'll need X-rays first and then we can tell exactly what we're dealing with. If her shoulder has popped out its socket it will need putting back before the nerves are damaged. You also need to check if the humerus is fractured. OK?'

Helen nodded, looking a little daunted at being put in charge of a patient. Mac watched as she hurried to the phone to request the services of the duty radiographer. She would manage fine, although he would keep a close eye on her. However, if she was to develop her skills then she needed to step up to the plate, as every young doctor had to do. He turned his attention to Ethan, checking his pulse and oxygen levels. Bailey Thomas, the Australian specialist resus nurse, was assisting him and

Mac nodded when he asked if Mac intended to aspirate.

'Yep. I reckon there's blood in the pleural cavity, don't you? Let's see if we can drain it off and help him breathe a bit easier.'

Bailey fetched what they needed and Mac set to work, easing the needle through the tough intercostal muscles between the boy's ribs. He was unsurprised when he immediately drew off bloody fluid. 'Definitely a haemothorax,' he said, glancing at Bailey. Out of the corner of his eye, he saw that the radiographer was putting Emily's X-rays up on the monitor. Even from where he was standing, Mac could see that the girl's humerus was fractured although he didn't say anything. He wanted Helen to find her feet and spotting the fracture herself would help her do that.

'Let's see if we can get any more out of there,' he said, turning back to Ethan. He aspirated some more blood before he was satisfied that he had alleviated the problem. Ethan's sats were back to what they should have been and he was breathing steadily so it was time to assess what other injuries he had sustained. Mac called over the radiographer and asked her to do a whole-body X-ray. While she was doing that he went to check on Helen.

'So, how's it going?' he asked, leaving her to explain her findings.

'It's as you suspected—the humerus is fractured at the upper end.' Helen pointed out the fracture and Mac nodded.

'So it is. Well spotted. Her shoulder's also dislocated so that needs sorting as well.'

'What should I do?' Helen asked uncertainly. 'Should I try to reduce the dislocation and pop the humerus back into its socket or what? I've not dealt with a case where the humerus is fractured as well.'

'It would be far too painful for Emily if we did it here. Plus there's the problem of the fracture, which complicates matters,' he explained. He always enjoyed helping the younger doctors and, unlike a lot of his peers, never considered it to be a waste of his time. The more everyone knew, the easier it was for the rest of the team, he reasoned.

'Phone Theatre and book her in ASAP. They'll take care of the lot and that way Emily won't know a thing about it. You just need to get her parents' permission for the operation to go ahead, so see if they've arrived yet and if not get the police to contact them. Tell them it's urgent.' He grinned at her. 'We don't want to waste any time so lay it on thick. It's the one time you're allowed to lie to the police!'

'Will do!' Helen was laughing as she hurried out of Resus to set the wheels turning.

Mac smiled as he went back to his patient. From what he had seen so far, Helen had the makings of a really good doctor. She would learn a lot from working here too. It made him suddenly glad that he had agreed to cover the paediatric A&E unit until their own registrar returned to work. Oh, he'd had his doubts when he had found out that Bella was working here. After everything that Tim had told him, it was only natural, although now he could see that he had been a little too hasty. OK, so maybe there had been a few teething problems but he and Bella seemed to be getting on remarkably well, all things considered.

The radiographer interrupted his thoughts just then to tell him the films were ready and he turned towards the monitor. There would be time enough to think about his relationship with Bella later.

Mac's heart skipped a beat. When had it turned into a relationship? It definitely hadn't been that before last night, had it? At the very most, he would have classed it as friendship— he and Bella were friends and that was it. However, deep down he knew it wasn't that any longer. At least not *only* that. Friendship had been hiked up to another level, to the point of becoming a relationship. He wasn't sure if that was a good thing or not, but he was powerless to do anything about it.

He took a deep breath as he stared at the screen. He and Bella had a relationship. Pick the bones out of that!

Bella squared her shoulders as she watched the taxi drive away from the hospital. She would collect her keys from Mac and head straight home. The sooner she was back in her apartment, the sooner she would be able to rid herself of the ridiculous notion of asking him if she could spend another night on the boat. Maybe it had helped to stay there last night, but she had to stand on her own two feet. She couldn't expect Mac to *mollycoddle* her.

She went straight to Reception, only to come to a halt when she saw all the children mill-ing around in the waiting area. It didn't take a genius to work out that something major must have happened so she made her way to the nursing station. Trish Baxter was adding more names to the whiteboard, squeezing them in around the edges. She grimaced when she saw Bella.

'We're fast running out of space. I'll have to resort to taping up a bit of paper soon!'

'What's happened?' Bella demanded, glancing at the list. From what she could see, there were fifteen children waiting to be seen, plus another six receiving treatment: three in cubicles, one in the treatment room, plus two more in Resus.

'A lorry ran into the bus taking the kids to the high school,' Trish explained. She put the cap back on the pen and placed it in the tray. 'To say it's been a tad chaotic in here this morning is an understatement.'

'I can imagine,' Bella agreed, shrugging off

her jacket. 'Right, who's next on the list? Freya Watson from the look of it,' she continued, answering her own question.

'I thought you were supposed to be off today,' Trish pointed out as they went back to Reception.

'I am. But I can't just take off and leave you to it when something like this has happened.' Bella picked up the girl's notes and looked around the waiting room. 'Freya Watson?' She smiled reassuringly when a tall red-haired girl hesitantly stood up. 'Come with me, Freya, and we'll get you sorted out.'

Bella led the girl to a cubicle. According to her notes, Freya was sixteen years old and in her last year at the high school. She looked extremely nervous as she sat down on the bed and Bella smiled encouragingly at her. 'This must have been a big shock for you. You're bound to feel rather shaken up and even a little bit tearful, but that's perfectly normal. I'm just going to check you over and make sure you're all right and then, as soon as your parents get here, you can go home.'

Freya didn't say anything as she stared down at the floor and Bella frowned. Although her notes stated that Freya appeared to have suffered only minor bruising, she couldn't rid herself of the feeling that there was something else wrong with her. She didn't say anything, however, as she set about examining her. If there was something wrong then it would soon become apparent. There was quite heavy bruising to the girl's thighs and it was obviously painful because she winced.

'How did this happen, do you know?' Bella asked, gently examining the area.

'A bag fell off the luggage rack and landed on me,' Freya muttered.

'I see. That must have hurt,' Bella said sympathetically. 'Can I just check your tummy?

I need to see if it's caused any bruising there as well.'

She went to unbutton the oversized cardigan that Freya was wearing but the girl pushed her hands away. There was real fear in her eyes when she looked at Bella.

'I'm all right!' she said sharply, attempting to stand up. The words were barely out of her mouth, however, when she doubled up in pain.

Bella caught her as she fell and eased her back down onto the bed. 'Obviously you're not all right, Freya, so I need to examine you. Come on, don't be silly. I only want to check that you're not badly injured.'

Tears started to stream down the girl's face as Bella unfastened her cardigan. As soon as she had done so, she realised what was wrong. Freya was pregnant and, from the look of her, at full term too. She chose her words with care, knowing how important it was that she gained the girl's trust.

'Do you know when your baby is due, Freya?'

'No. Not really. I just kept hoping it wasn't actually happening.' She looked up and Bella's heart ached when she saw the fear in her eyes. 'My mum and dad are going to kill me when they find out! They're always banging on about me not getting myself into any trouble.'

'I'm sure they will be fine once they get over the shock,' Bella said soothingly, mentally crossing her fingers.

She quickly examined the girl, her heart sinking when she realised that the baby's head was engaged. As she'd suspected, Freya was at full term and, when she let out a groan, Bella realised that there was no time to waste; the baby was about to be born. Hurrying to the phone, she rang Maternity and asked them to send over a midwife as soon as possible. In the meantime, she would have to manage as best she could, although it was a long time since she had delivered a baby. Poking her head out of the cubicle, she beckoned to Trish, who had just finished seeing her patient. She lowered her voice, not wanting anyone to overhear. Although there was little hope of keeping the baby's arrival a secret for very long, at least Freya should be able to tell her parents before her classmates found out.

'We've a bit of a situation in here. It turns out that Freya is pregnant and the baby is on its way. I've asked for a midwife to attend but I don't know how long it will be before she gets here, so we're going to have to manage as best we can. Can we move her into Resus to give her some privacy? Apparently her parents have no idea that she's pregnant.'

'Blooming heck!' Trish exclaimed. 'I know her parents and, believe me, they're going to have a fit when they find out. They're very strait-laced, from what I know of them. Pity help the poor kid is all I can say.'

'Great!' Bella sighed. 'I'll get onto Social

Services as soon as I can, but my main concern right now is keeping a lid on this so that the rest of the school doesn't find out. Has Mac finished in Resus, do you know?'

'I'll go and check. Won't be a sec.'

Trish hurried away as Bella went back into the cubicle. Freya was moaning softly and clutching her stomach, obviously in the throes of labour. Bella checked her over once again, grimacing when she discovered that Freya's cervix was fully dilated. From the look of her, it wouldn't be long before the baby arrived.

'It shouldn't be long before your baby is born,' she told her gently. 'I know it hurts, sweetheart, but once the midwife gets here she'll sort out some pain relief for you. Do you understand what happens when a baby is born?'

Freya nodded. 'We did it in biology, how the cervix has to dilate and soften so that the baby can make its way out of the birth canal.'

'Good. At least you have some idea of what's happening and that will help.'

Bella looked round when she heard the curtain open, feeling her heart leap when she saw Mac coming into the cubicle. Although it was barely an hour since they had parted, it was as though she was seeing him through fresh eyes. Her gaze ran over him, taking stock of the dark brown hair falling over his forehead, the midnight blue of his eyes, the strongly masculine set to his features. There was no doubt at all that Mac was an extremely attractive man and she couldn't understand why she had never realised it before…

Her breath caught as she was suddenly forced to confront the truth. Deep down, she had always been aware of his appeal, only she had been too afraid to admit it.

CHAPTER FIVE

FREYA'S BABY ARRIVED just twenty minutes later. It was a little girl and she was absolutely perfect in every way, despite the fact that her mother had received no antenatal care. Mac gently placed the little mite in her mother's arms, wondering what was going to happen now. Bella had explained the situation to him and although he understood what a shock it was going to be for Freya's parents, surely they would support their daughter during this difficult time?

He sighed, realising that it could be wishful thinking. He only had to recall what had happened to his own mother to know that the happily-ever-after scenario wasn't guaranteed.

His maternal grandparents had refused to have anything to do with his mother after he had been born. As his father had been brought up in care and hadn't had any contact with his family, it had meant that his parents had had to struggle along on their own. Although his dad had done his best, his lack of qualifications had meant that he'd had to take a series of low-paid jobs, so money had been tight. Coming from a comfortable middle-class background, his mother had found it very difficult to adapt to the change in lifestyle, so it wasn't surprising that she had left.

'The midwife should be here shortly.' Bella came back from phoning the maternity unit. 'Apparently they're short-staffed and that's why it's taken them so long to send anyone over here. However, they've promised to get a midwife to us as soon as they can.'

'Not much they can do now,' Mac replied laconically, trying not to think about how much he had missed his mother after she had left. It was all water under the bridge and had no bearing on his life these days.

'No, I suppose not. I'm only glad that you were here. It's been ages since I delivered a baby and I'm rather rusty, I'm afraid.'

'I've delivered my share over the past few years,' he said wryly, returning his thoughts to the matter at hand. After all, he'd had his father, hadn't he? So he'd been far luckier than a lot of kids. 'You have to turn your hand to most things when you're working overseas.'

'Well, all the practice definitely stood you in good stead today.' She smiled but there was a wariness about the look she gave him that made Mac wonder if something had upset her. However, before he could attempt to find out, Trish popped her head round the door.

'Mr and Mrs Watson are here. How do you want to play this, Bella? Shall I show them straight in here or do you want a word with them first?'

'I'd better have a word with them first,' Bella replied with a sigh. She turned to Mac after Trish left. 'I'll send Jenny in to sit with Freya. You must have loads to do.'

'I need to check how many kids are still waiting to be seen,' Mac agreed, following her to the door. He looked back and frowned as he watched Freya cradling her baby. 'It's going to be a massive shock for her parents so let's hope they can rise to the occasion. That girl is going to need a lot of support in the coming months.'

'She is,' Bella agreed soberly. 'Having a baby at her age is a lot to cope with.'

'It is. My parents were only a year or so older than Freya when they had me.' He opened the door but he could sense Bella's curiosity as she stepped out into the corridor and suddenly wished that he hadn't said anything. Maybe it was the birth of the baby or thinking about his parents, but he was very aware that his emotions were rather too near the surface for comfort.

'I didn't know that your parents were so young when you were born,' she said quietly as they made their way to Reception.

'There's no reason why you should have known,' he countered. 'It's not something that came up in conversation, I imagine.'

'No. Probably not.' She hesitated. 'It must have been difficult for them, though. Did your grandparents help?'

'Nope. Dad was brought up in care and he'd lost touch with his family. As for my mother, well, her parents took the view that she'd made her decision and it was up to her to live with the consequences. They wanted her to have a termination, apparently, but she wouldn't hear of it,' he added when Bella looked at him questioningly. 'They refused to have anything more to do with her after that.'

'Really? Oh, how awful for her!' She touched his arm and he could see the sympathy in her eyes. 'And awful for you, too.'

'I survived.' Mac dredged up a smile, afraid that he would do something really stupid. Maybe it did hurt to know that his grandparents had turned their backs on him but he was far too old to start crying about it at this stage! He swung round, determined that he wasn't going to make a fool of himself. Maybe Bella *had* touched a chord but there was no way that he intended to let her know that. 'Right, I'll go and check how we're doing. Catch you later.'

'I expect so.'

There was a faintly wistful note in her voice but Mac refused to speculate on the reason for it. He went to the desk and checked how many children were still waiting to be seen. There were just half a dozen left so he took the next one to the cubicles and got him sorted out. While his mind was busily engaged it couldn't start wandering, could it? he reasoned.

He sighed, uncomfortably aware that he had never experienced this problem before. He wasn't someone who wore his heart on his sleeve and yet the minute Bella had expressed her sympathy, he had turned to mush. What was happening to him? First there had been all those crazy thoughts he'd had last night—the ones that had involved him, Bella, and a bed—and now this. He had to get a grip. Maybe Bella *did* make him feel things he had never felt before but he had to remember that, to all intents and purposes, she still belonged to Tim. No way was he going to be responsible for Tim suffering a relapse! No, Bella was off limits. She always had been and she always would be too.

It was almost lunchtime before Bella felt that she could leave. The last of the children had been seen and sent home and the department was more or less back to normal. Granted, there was a lot of paperwork that still needed doing, but she felt that she could justifiably leave that to Mac. After all, it was supposed to be her day off and there was no reason to feel guilty about going home. It was only when she was halfway across the car park that she remembered that she had forgotten to ask Mac for her keys.

She sighed as she turned round and headed back. She could have done without having to speak to him again, if she was honest. What he had told her earlier in the day about his family had affected her far more than she would have expected. She couldn't help thinking how hard it must have been for him to grow up knowing that he had been rejected by his grandparents.

Bella gave herself a mental shake as she reached the main doors leading into the hospital. She had to stop thinking about Mac all

the time. Maybe she did feel incredibly aware
of him, but she couldn't afford to let it take
over her life the way it was doing. The sooner
she got it into her head that he was just a col-
league, the simpler it would be.

She was just about to enter the hospital when
Mac himself appeared. He smiled ruefully as
he held up her car keys.

'You need these, don't you? Sorry! I should
have handed them back before.'

'Don't worry about it.'

Bella dredged up a smile as she took the keys
off him but it was hard to behave naturally.
Why had she never noticed before what a gor-
geous shade of blue his eyes were, like the sky
on a summer evening? And how come she had
never realised just how tall he was, not to mention how lean and fit his body looked? Her
thoughts skittered this way and that so that it
was a moment before she realised that he had
asked her a question.

'Sorry,' she said hurriedly. 'What did you say?'

'I was just wondering how it went with Freya's parents.'

Bella felt a shiver ripple through her at the sound of his deep voice. She had to make a conscious effort not to show the effect it was having on her. If she hadn't noticed his eyes or his physique before then she certainly hadn't noticed how seductive his voice sounded!

'Not too good, I'm afraid. They wouldn't believe me at first, insisted that it couldn't be their daughter and that there must have been a mix-up with the names. Then when I took them in to see Freya, they lost it completely and started shouting at her.' She sighed, deliberately reining in her wayward thoughts. 'It was so bad, in fact, that I had to ask them to leave in the end.'

'Sounds grim. How did Freya take it?'

'Pretty much as you'd expect. It took me ages

to calm her down but it's a lot to deal with at her age.'

'It is. What's going to happen when she leaves hospital? Are her parents going to take her home and support her?'

'I doubt it, from what I heard.' Bella shrugged. 'I've spoken to Social Services and they've promised to visit her. They said that they will arrange accommodation for her and the baby when she's discharged. In the unlikely event that Mr and Mrs Watson change their minds, they will cancel the arrangements.'

'I'm not sure which is worse,' Mac said grimly. 'Being dumped in some grotty flat or going home and being faced with constant re-criminations. That won't do her or the child any good, will it?'

'It won't. But there's not much we can do except pray for a miracle,' Bella said sadly.

'Pray that Freya's parents will have a change of heart, you mean?' He shook his head. 'In my experience, it rarely happens so I wouldn't hold out too many hopes on that score.'

'Your grandparents never changed their minds?' Bella said quietly, hearing the echo of pain in his voice.

'No. Oh, Mum tried to persuade them to see sense, but they were adamant that they wanted nothing to do with her or me. I never met them, in fact.'

'How sad. Not just for you and your mother, but for them too. They could have had the pleasure of watching you grow up if they hadn't taken such a rigid stance.'

'Obviously, they didn't see it that way. The shame of their unmarried daughter having a baby outweighed everything else.'

'I can't understand why people feel like that,' Bella admitted. 'Oh, I know my parents were more interested in their careers than in me, but I'd like to think they would have supported me if I'd found myself in that position.'

'There wasn't much chance of that happening, though, was there?' Mac observed drily.

Bella's brows rose. 'What do you mean?'

'Nothing. Forget it. Right, I'd better get back. Thanks again for the loan of your car.'

He started to go back inside but Bella knew that she couldn't let him leave without explaining that cryptic comment. She caught hold of his arm, feeling a flutter of awareness run through her as she felt the warmth of his skin seep through her fingertips. It was all she could do not to release him immediately, but she needed to know what he had meant.

'I want to know what you meant,' she said firmly, determined that she was going to put a lid on all these crazy feelings. All she was doing was touching his arm, for heaven's sake, not making mad, passionate love with him! The thought wasn't the best she could have come up with, but she stood her ground. For some reason it seemed vitally important that she found out what he was talking about. 'Well?'

'Tim told me that you'd refused to have a baby.' His eyes met hers and she felt chilled to the core when she saw the condemnation they held. 'It was obvious how upset he was and I don't blame him. Having a child could have been exactly what he needed to keep him on track.'

'Is that what Tim told you? Or is that your expert opinion?' Bella laughed harshly, more hurt than she could say. Once again Mac was blaming her for what had happened and it was even more hurtful after last night. She'd thought that he was starting to accept that she wasn't solely at fault for the demise of her marriage but she'd been wrong. All of a sudden the need to set him straight overcame everything else.

'Don't bother answering that—it really doesn't matter. The only thing that matters is why I refused to have a baby. I don't suppose Tim explained that, did he?' She didn't give him a chance to answer. 'I refused because there was no way that I was bringing a child into the world who wasn't really wanted. Oh, maybe Tim claimed that he wanted a baby but he only wanted one *after* I told him I was leaving him. He'd always refused to start a family before that, told me that he had no intention of having children when they would only tie him down. However, once I asked him for a divorce, he changed his mind.'

She stared back at him, wondering if he would believe her. Maybe he would and maybe he wouldn't, but she intended to tell him the truth. What he made of it was up to him. 'I refused point-blank and I don't give a damn if you think I was wrong to do so. There was no way that I was prepared to have a baby just to try and save our marriage. That was well and truly over, believe me!'

She swung round, ignoring Mac's demands for her to stop. Walking over to her car, she got in and drove out of the car park without a backward glance. She wasn't sure how she felt, if she was honest, whether she was more angry than hurt by his continued refusal to believe that she wasn't solely to blame. However, what she did know was that she wouldn't make the mistake of thinking that he was on her side ever again. Maybe it had appeared that way last night but it wasn't true. Mac's loyalties didn't lie with her but with Tim. It just proved how little he really cared about her, despite his claims to the contrary.

Mac felt absolutely dreadful for the rest of the day. He couldn't rid himself of the memory of how hurt Bella had looked as she had driven away. By the time his shift ended, he knew that he couldn't leave things the way they were. He had to see her and clear the air. If he could.

He collected his motorbike and headed into the town centre. He had got Bella's address from the staff files and knew that she lived in one of the new apartments that had been built on the site of the old brewery. He'd heard that the cost of renting an apartment there was extremely steep, not that it would worry Bella, of course. She was in the fortunate position of having a private income and it was yet another reminder of why he needed to quash any fanciful thoughts he might be harbouring. Although he earned a decent salary, he wasn't in Bella's league!

Mac parked the motorbike and walked to the entrance. There was an intercom system so he pressed the bell, steeling himself when he heard her voice coming through the speaker. He wouldn't blame her if she refused to see him, but he really and truly needed to sort this out.

'Bella, it's me—Mac. I need a word with you.'

'I'm afraid now isn't a good time,' she began,

but he didn't let her finish. He had a nasty feeling that if he didn't resolve this issue tonight, he might never be able to do so. If Tim had lied to him then he needed to know.

'I understand that you're angry but we need to sort this out, Bella, once and for all.'

'Why?' She gave a harsh little laugh and his insides twisted when he heard the pain in her voice. 'What difference will it make to you if Tim was spinning you a line? You're still going to take his side, aren't you, still going to blame me for ending our marriage? As far as you're concerned, Mac, I should have stuck with him come hell or high water, so what's the point of talking about it?'

'The point is that I need to know the truth.' Mac took a deep breath, aware that he was stepping into dangerous territory, yet how could he avoid it? Bella deserved to be given a fair hearing and that was what he intended to do. If she would agree. 'I know it's asking a lot but, please, Bella, let me in so we can talk this all through.'

He held his breath, hoping against hope that he had managed to persuade her. When he heard the door lock being released, he almost shouted out loud in relief. He hurried inside and made straight for the lift, half afraid that she would change her mind. Her apartment was on the fifth floor and he tapped his foot in impatience as the lift carried him upwards. He wasn't sure how he was going to set about this; maybe it would be simpler just to wait and see how it panned out? If he started asking questions, there was always a chance that he would say something to alienate her. He sighed as the lift came to a halt. Normally, he wouldn't have given it a second thought; he would have simply asked Bella what had gone on and that would have been it. But this wasn't a normal situation, was it? Someone was lying and he needed to find out who it was.

Bella must have heard the lift stop because she opened the door. She didn't say a word, however, as she led the way inside the apartment. Mac placed his motorbike helmet on the console table in the foyer then followed her into the living room, stopping abruptly when he was greeted by the most spectacular sight. One whole wall was made of glass and the view of the mountains that surrounded the town was stupendous.

'What a fabulous view!' He went over to the window and stood there for a moment, drinking it in. It was only when he became aware of the silence that he remembered why he had come. He turned slowly around, his heart aching when he saw how distant Bella looked. She had always had a tendency to withdraw into herself if something had upset her and it was obvious that was happening now.

'Thank you for letting me in,' Mac said quietly, trying to rein in the guilt he felt. It didn't make him feel good to know that he had upset her, even though it hadn't been intentional. He sighed, aware that he could make the situation worse if he continued probing, but what choice did he have? He needed to get at the truth.

'What you told me before about Tim not wanting a child until you asked him for a divorce—was it true?' he said before his courage deserted him.

'Yes. Not that I expect you to believe me.'

Mac heard the challenge in her voice but it didn't disguise the pain it held as well and his heart ached all the more. That she was loath to discuss what had gone on was obvious and in other circumstances he wouldn't have pushed her. However, making sure that he could trust her was even more important than finding out if Tim had lied to him.

The thought stunned him because it aroused feelings that he'd believed he had conquered many years before. After his mother had left, he had found it impossible to trust anyone. He had been only seven when Laura MacIntyre had walked out of their home but he could still remember how terrified he had been in case his father had left him as well.

Was that why he had avoided commitment? he wondered suddenly. Was it the reason why he always called time on a relationship before it became too serious? He was afraid of letting himself fall in love in case he was let down. His breath caught as one thought led to another: was it also the reason why it was so important that he made sure he could trust Bella?

Mac felt panic assail him when he realised just how complicated the situation actually was. His feelings for Bella weren't nearly as clear-cut as he had believed. They seemed to be changing on a daily basis, in fact. He had started out feeling disillusioned, angry even about the way she had behaved, yet he couldn't put his hand on his heart and swear that was how he felt now.

A trickle of sweat ran down his back as he looked at her and remembered how he had felt the night before, how he had ached to touch her, kiss her, feel her body, warm and responsive under his. It certainly hadn't been anger or disillusionment he had felt then!

Bella wasn't sure what Mac was thinking but there was something about the way he was looking at her that made her heart start to race. She bit her lip, determined that she was going to keep a lid on her emotions. If they were to sort this out then she had to remain detached. She had told Mac her version of what had happened, the *true* version, and now it was up to him to decide if he believed her. The one thing she mustn't do was get emotionally involved. Something warned her that would be a mistake of gigantic proportions.

Turning, she went over to the drinks trolley and poured a little brandy into a couple of crystal glasses. Although she rarely drank spirits, she felt in need of some Dutch courage to see her through the next few minutes. Walking over to one of the huge black leather sofas, she sat down, placing the drinks on the glass-and-steel coffee table. She had rented the apartment fully furnished and hadn't made any changes to it. It was merely a place to eat and sleep when she got back from work, yet all of a sudden she found herself wondering what Mac would make of it. Having experienced the welcoming warmth of his boat, she couldn't imagine that it would appeal to him on any level.

For some reason she found the idea upsetting but she refused to dwell on it. It wasn't her taste in furnishings that Mac was interested in but her honesty! Anger rippled through her as she picked up a glass and took a sip of the brandy. She had done nothing wrong and the sooner he accepted that the better.

'So, seeing as you've seen fit to come here to talk to me, I suggest you get on with it.' Bella stared at him over the rim of the glass, wanting to make it clear that she didn't intend to allow this to drag on. She had been genuinely upset when she had got home but she'd had time to calm down now and she had no intention of getting upset again, no matter what he thought. *She* knew she was telling the truth and that was what mattered, wasn't it?

She clamped down on the tiny flicker of doubt, knowing how quickly it could turn into something much bigger. Mac came and sat down opposite her, although he didn't make any attempt to pick up his glass. He stared down at the floor for a moment and her heart surged when she saw how grim he looked when he finally raised his head.

'Why would Tim lie to me, though? That's

what I don't understand.' He pinned her with a look of such intensity that she was hard-pressed not to look away, but somehow she managed to hold his gaze.

'You'll have to ask him that.'

'But doesn't it make you angry that he's blaming you for everything that happened?' he retorted.

'Yes, it does.' Bella managed to suppress a shiver when she heard the anger in his voice. Was he angry because Tim had lied to him or because he didn't believe her? She had no idea but she couldn't afford to let it worry her, certainly couldn't allow it to unleash all the emotions that were churning around inside her.

'Then how can you sit there so calmly? Surely, you want to do something to address the situation, Bella.'

'What do you suggest? That I contact everyone I know and tell them that Tim is lying?' She gave a bitter little laugh. 'Maybe some people will believe me, but not very many, I'm afraid. Most will take Tim's side simply because he's always been far more outgoing than me. I have a tendency to keep myself to myself, and that doesn't help if you're trying to get people on your side. I mean, even you aren't sure who to believe, are you, Mac? And you know me better than anyone else does.'

CHAPTER SIX

MAC FELT HIS blood pressure rocket skywards. Bella thought that he knew her better than anyone else? Coming on top of everything that had happened recently, it was almost too much to take in and yet he couldn't pretend that he didn't experience a rush of pleasure at the idea. Knowing Bella, inside and out, was his dearest wish.

'Which is why I want to get to the bottom of this.' He cleared his throat when he realised how uptight he sounded. Until he was sure who was telling the truth, he needed to remain impartial. The thought of how easily he could be swayed by all the emotions rampaging around inside him was sobering. Mac deliberately cleared his head of everything else while he focused on the reason why he had come to see her.

'So you're just going to leave things the way they are and not try to defend yourself?'

'Basically, yes.' She sighed. 'I can't see any point in making a fuss, if I'm honest. Tim obviously has his reasons for blaming me and, quite frankly, I don't intend to end up having a public slanging match with him to clear my name. *I* know what really happened and that's what matters most of all.'

'So what you're saying is that you don't care what anyone else thinks,' Mac said slowly. He shook his head. 'That doesn't seem fair to me. I mean, why should everyone believe you're to blame when it wasn't your fault?'

'It's just the way things are.' Bella shrugged, trying not to get too hung up on the thought that Mac must care if he was so keen to straighten things out. She'd been down that route last night and she wasn't about to make the same mistake again. Maybe Mac did care but out of a sense of justice: it wasn't personal.

'Maybe Tim finds it easier to deal with what's happened by blaming me,' she said flatly, not wanting to dwell on the thought when it evoked so many mixed feelings. She and Mac had never been more than friends and it would be stupid to think that their relationship had changed. 'After all, he's been through a very difficult time. Dealing with his addiction can't have been easy for him. You know as well as I do how hard it is for an addict to get clean and stay off the drugs.'

'Yes, I do.' His tone was flat. 'I grew up in an area where drugs were part of everyday life, so I understand the damage they cause. That Tim managed to overcome his addiction is to his credit but it still doesn't excuse what he's doing, going around telling everyone a pack of lies. He needs to accept responsibility for his actions. Then maybe there's a chance that you two can get back together.'

'That isn't going to happen,' Bella said quietly. 'Our marriage is over and there's no chance of us trying again.'

'But you must still have feelings for him. Oh, I know it's been tough, Bella. Probably tougher for you than it was for Tim, in fact, because he was more concerned about where his next fix was coming from.' He leant forward and she could see the urgency in his eyes. 'But you loved him once, otherwise you wouldn't have married him, would you? So why not give it another shot?'

'As I said, it isn't going to happen.'

She stood up, wanting to make it clear that she didn't intend to discuss the matter any further. She and Tim were never getting back together for one simple reason: she didn't love him and she never had loved him either.

The thought was incredibly painful as it seemed to highlight how out of touch she was with her own emotions. As she led the way to the door, Bella felt a wave of despair wash over her. How could she ever trust her own judgement again? How could she be sure if she did fall in love that it was the real thing this time? The thought of living out her life in a state of lonely uncertainty was more than she could bear, especially with Mac there—Mac, who always seemed so sure of himself, so confident about what he wanted. She couldn't imagine Mac experiencing all these crippling doubts!

Bella opened the door, her heart aching as she fixed a smile to her lips. 'Thank you for coming. I'll see you in work, I expect.'

'So that's it, is it? I've said my piece and you've said yours and that's the end of the matter?' His dark brows drew together as he glowered down at her.

'I can't think of anything else that we need

to say.' She gave a little shrug, aiming for a nonchalance she wished she felt. Maybe it was silly, but she had always dreamt of finding the right man and falling in love. However, it seemed unlikely that it would happen now. 'I've told you my side of the story and now it's up to you to decide who you believe.'

'In other words, you don't give a damn if I think you're lying.' He laughed harshly, so harshly that she flinched. 'I have to hand it to you, Bella. Your self-confidence is amazing!'

'You're wrong. I don't feel confident at all,' she shot back. 'I have no idea if you believe me, Mac, but what can I do about it? Should I try to convince you by telling you about all the horrible things Tim said to me or all the lies he told? Should I tell you about his affair to try and gain your sympathy?' She shook her head. 'Sorry, but it isn't going to happen. Either you believe me or you don't—it's as simple as that.'

'Affair? What do you mean? What affair?'

The shock in his voice cut through her anger. Bella bit her lip, wishing she hadn't told him that. It hadn't been intentional, but the words had somehow slipped out.

'It doesn't matter…' she began.

'Of course it matters!' He gripped hold of her by the shoulders as he bent to look into her eyes, and maybe it was the fact that she was feeling so wrung out, but all of a sudden she couldn't contain her feelings any longer. Tears began to pour down her face and she heard him groan.

'Oh, Bella, I'm sorry! I didn't mean to upset you.' He drew her to him, cradling her against the solid strength of his body, and she cried all the harder. It had been such a long time since anyone had held her like this, since anyone had cared.

'Shh. It's OK, sweetheart. Don't cry. Everything's going to be fine, I promise you.'

He drew her closer, running his hand down her back in a gesture that was meant simply to comfort, and she sighed. She could feel his fingers gliding down her spine, warm and wonderfully soothing as they traced the delicate column of bones. His hand reached the curve of her buttocks and stopped. Bella could feel the heat of his fingers burning through her clothing and shuddered. All of a sudden the air seemed thick with tension, filled with a sense of anticipation that immediately dried her tears. She realised that she was holding her breath as she waited to see what would happen...

His hand slid back up, following the route it had already travelled. When it reached the nape of her neck it stopped again, resting lightly beneath the heavy knot of her hair. Bella bit her lip, suddenly unsure about what she should do. Should she break the contact, step away from him and make it clear that she didn't welcome this kind of intimacy? But surely that would be a lie? Having Mac hold her, caress her, make her feel all these things *was* what she wanted.

Desperately.

Helplessly, her eyes rose to his and she felt her heart lurch when she saw the awareness on his face. She knew in that moment that Mac understood how confused she felt because he felt the same. Maybe it was that thought, that single mind-blowing thought, that unlocked all her reservations, but she didn't pause to consider what she was doing as she reached up and drew his head down. Their mouths met, clung, and it was like nothing she had experienced before. There was desire, yes, but there was so much more to the kiss than passion. The feel of Mac's mouth on hers made her feel safe, secure, protected. It was as though she had found her way back home after a long and exhausting journey.

Bella wasn't sure how long the kiss lasted. It

could have been seconds or a lifetime for all she knew. She was trembling when they finally broke apart, but so was Mac. He ran the pad of his thumb over her swollen lips and his eyes were alight with a tenderness that filled her with warmth. It was obvious that she wasn't the only one to have been so deeply moved by what had happened.

'I didn't plan this, Bella, but I'm not sorry it happened and I hope you aren't either?'

His voice was low, deep, and she shivered when she heard the desire it held. She had done this to him, she thought in amazement. She had aroused his passion and it was a revelation to realise that she was capable of making him want her this much.

'I'm not. I'm not sorry at all,' she said in a husky little voice that made his eyes darken. When he reached out and pulled her back into his arms, she knew what was going to happen. Maybe they hadn't planned it, but there was no point pretending. They had both thought about it—thought about how it would feel to lie in each other's arms and make love. And tonight it was going to happen.

When he swung her up into his arms and carried her into the bedroom, she didn't protest. Why would she when it was what she wanted so much? He laid her down on the huge bed and sat down beside her, his hand trembling just a little as he cupped her cheek.

'Are you sure, Bella? Absolutely certain this is what you want?'

'Yes.' She captured his hand, gently biting the pad of flesh at the base of his thumb, and didn't even feel shocked by her own temerity. This was Mac and whatever happened between them tonight felt right. 'I'm sure, Mac. Completely and utterly sure.'

He made a sound deep in his throat as he stood up and started to strip off his clothes. His body was lean and fit, the muscles in his chest flexing as he dragged his T-shirt over his head and tossed it onto the floor. Bella's eyes ran over him, greedily drinking in the sight of his body, so beautiful in its masculinity. She bit her lip as her gaze came to rest on his erection because there was little doubt about how much he wanted her. Her eyes rose to his and she realised that she must be blushing when he laughed softly and tenderly.

'It's hard for a man to hide how he feels. When he wants a woman as much as I want you, Bella, then it's pretty obvious, I'm afraid.'

'Don't apologise,' she said with a bravado that would have shocked her once upon a time but felt completely natural now. She laughed up at him. 'It's good to know that it isn't all one-sided.'

'Oh, it most definitely isn't!' He lay down on the bed and gathered her into his arms while he kissed her with a passion that made her tingle both inside and out. Propping himself up on his elbow, he smiled into her eyes. 'You're a great kisser, Bella English. I have no complaints on that score.'

'Thank you,' she retorted. 'I hope you don't have any complaints on any other score, either.'

'Maybe just one.' He kissed the tip of her nose and grinned at her. 'You're decidedly overdressed for what I have in mind. Still, it shouldn't take long to resolve the problem.'

His hands went to the buttons on her shirt and Bella sighed. Her lack of experience hadn't prepared her for his relaxed approach to lovemaking. Passion was tempered by humour and, amazingly, that only seemed to heighten her desire for him. By the time he reached the final button, she was trembling with need but it was obvious that he didn't intend to rush things.

He parted the edges of her shirt with exquisite slowness and stared down at her breasts, barely concealed by the lacy white bra she was wearing. His eyes were filled with so many emotions when he looked up that her heart overflowed. Was this how it should be? she wondered giddily. Was this what she had missed, having a man look at her as though she was the most wonderful sight he had ever seen? She had no idea what the answer was but she knew that she would remember this moment for the rest of her life—the moment when she discovered how it really felt to be a woman.

'You're so beautiful, Bella. So very, very beautiful...'

The rest of the words were swallowed up as he bent and drew her nipple into his mouth. Bella cried out at the explosion of sensations that erupted inside her. The moist heat of his tongue, the erotic stimulation of the damp lace against her flesh, the sensual whisper of his breath as he raised his head and blew gently on the hard nub made her tremble with long-ing. When he turned his attention to her other breast, lavishing it with the same attention, she wasn't sure if she could bear it. She could feel her passion mounting, feel her desire growing more and more urgent with every delicate stroke of his tongue. Lacing her fingers through his hair, she raised his head, uncaring if he could tell how much she needed him.

'Mac, I don't know if I can take much more of this,' she whispered hoarsely.

'Sweetheart!' He kissed her hard and hungrily, then stripped off the rest of her clothes until she was naked to his gaze. His eyes grazed over her and she shivered when she saw the desire they held as he raised his head. 'Tonight is going to be special, Bella. I promise you that. Just give me a second.'

He slid off the bed and, picking up his trousers, took out his wallet and removed a condom from it. Bella closed her eyes as he lay down beside her again and took her in his arms, shuddering as he entered her. There wasn't a doubt in her mind that he was right. Tonight *was* going to be special. For both of them.

Mac lay on his back, one arm resting across his eyes. It was almost midnight and the daylight had disappeared a long time ago, but they hadn't switched on the lamps. Maybe they had both felt a need to preserve the status quo. Casting light onto the scene might spoil things; it might make them question the wisdom of what they had done. He didn't want to do that and he sensed that Bella didn't want to do it either.

He sighed softly. He was still finding it difficult to accept how quickly his feelings had changed. The anger he had felt about the way Bella had treated Tim seemed to have melted away. Finding out that his friend had had an affair had been a shock but it wasn't only that which had made him see that he had been unfair to her. Holding her in his arms, being close to her had done more than merely satisfy his desire for her. It had made him remember exactly who she was, and that certainly wasn't the sort of woman who would turn her back on someone in need. No, Bella had been forced into ending her marriage by Tim's appalling behaviour and it made him feel incredibly guilty to know how badly he had misjudged her. Now he could only pray that he hadn't made her life even more difficult by what they had done.

'Penny for them, Dr MacIntyre.'

Her voice was low but Mac heard the uncertainty it held and lowered his arm. Rolling onto his side, he pulled her to him and kissed her softly on the lips. Maybe he did have doubts, but he intended to keep them to himself. He didn't want her worrying unnecessarily.

'I'm not sure they're worth as much as a penny,' he countered, clamping down on the rush of desire that flooded through him. They had made love not once but twice and he really shouldn't be feeling this need again, he told himself sternly, but to very little effect. 'I was just letting my mind drift rather than thinking actual thoughts.'

'So you weren't regretting what we've done?' She looked steadily into his eyes and he sighed, unable to lie to her.

'No. I don't regret it, but I do wonder if it was right. I…well, I don't want it to affect our friendship, Bella, and make life even more complicated for you.'

'Neither do I.'

She smiled but there was something about her expression that made him wonder if he had phrased that badly. Getting into a discussion about the problems it could cause if they had an affair didn't seem right, but maybe he should have made his feelings clearer? However, before he could try to make amends, she tossed back the quilt and stood up. Mac gulped as he was treated to a tantalising glimpse of her beautiful body before she pulled on a robe.

'I'll have a shower then make us some coffee. There's a second bathroom along the corridor if you want to use that,' she told him briskly.

'Thanks.'

Mac stayed where he was until she had disappeared into the en-suite bathroom. Getting out of bed, he gathered up his clothes and made his way to the bathroom. There was a heavy feeling in his heart, a suspicion that he had upset her, and he hated to think that his clumsiness had caused her any pain, but what should he do? Sit her down and explain how awkward he felt about encroaching on Tim's territory?

Although Bella had claimed that there was no chance of her and Tim getting back together, she could change her mind. He had seen it happen to other couples, watched as time had softened the bad memories and brought the good ones into focus. He wouldn't want to stand in the way of that happening. Neither would he want to be left with a broken heart if it did. If Bella did rediscover her love for Tim then how would it affect him?

Once again the fear of finding himself rejected reared its ugly head. As Mac got dressed, he tried his best to rationalise it away. He was a grown man, after all, not a scared seven-year-old child, and if anything happened he would deal with it. However, no matter how he tried to reason the fear away, it wouldn't budge. In all those dark places he didn't visit very often, he knew that losing Bella would be far worse than anything that had happened to him before. Once he had allowed himself to fall in love with her, his heart would no longer be his. It would belong exclusively to her.

Bella had the coffee ready by the time Mac appeared. She loaded everything on to a tray and carried it through to the sitting room. He was standing by the window, ostensibly enjoying the view, but she sensed that his thoughts were far removed from the charms of the moonlit scene. Was he afraid that he had allowed his judgement to be swayed by passion? Was he worried in case she had used sex as a means to convince him of her innocence? That thought stung more than any other could have done. The only reason she had slept with him was because she had wanted to!

She plonked the tray on the table with a thud that made him swing round and she felt her heart scrunch up in her chest when she saw the strain on his face. Whatever thoughts he was harbouring obviously weren't pleasant ones. Picking up the pot, she poured coffee into the mugs, wishing that some passing genie would spirit her away. She wasn't up to this! She couldn't face the thought of explaining why she had slept with him when it was obvious that her reasons were a world removed from his. Oh, so maybe he had wanted her; she'd seen definite proof of that! However, it meant nothing if he now regretted what they had done.

Bella's hand shook as she put the pot back on the tray. She couldn't believe how painful it was to know that Mac wished tonight had never happened. It felt like another rejection, just like the way Tim had rejected her when he'd had that affair. What was wrong with her? Was it her inability to show her emotions that drove men away?

That was what Tim had said during one of those terrible rows they'd had. He had accused her of being so cold that she had driven him into the arms of another woman. He had even blamed her coldness for his drug addiction and, although Bella knew that he had been trying to excuse his behaviour by blaming her, the words had stuck in her mind. Now they rose to the surface again to taunt her.

She was incapable of showing her true emotions because there was something missing from her make-up, some vital element she was lacking. No wonder Mac was having second thoughts about what had happened tonight. After all, what man would want to get involved with someone like her? Someone who wasn't a *real* woman.

Mac drank his coffee as quickly as he could. It was scalding hot but, he gulped it down anyway, uncaring if it burnt his tongue. He needed to get away and the sooner the better, preferably. He had never gone in for the *wham, bam, thank you, ma'am* routine; he'd had far too much respect for the women he had slept with to treat them that way. However, he would have given his right arm to simply cut and run without offering up any explanations. If he started to explain to Bella why he wanted to leave so desperately, who knew what he'd end up admitting? The thought of laying his soul bare gave him hot and cold chills and he stood up abruptly. He had to leave. Right now, this very second. No matter what Bella thought of him!

'I have to go.'

He headed for the door, hating himself for leaving her like this, yet unable to do anything about it. He knew that he was within a hair's breadth of falling in love with her and the thought scared him witless. It was all very well telling himself that he could cope with anything that happened, but could he if it involved losing Bella? Could he honestly see himself carrying on if he loved and subsequently lost her? Just the thought made his head spin, round and round, faster and faster, until it felt as though his thoughts were swirling on a merry-go-round. Losing Bella would be the one thing he couldn't handle, the thing that would bring him down, and he couldn't take that risk.

He stopped when he reached the front door, forcing himself to smile as he turned to her. His heart stuttered to a halt when he saw the pain in her eyes but he had to be strong, had to do what was right for her as well as right for him. It wasn't just himself he had to think about, after all. How Bella was going to feel was even more important. He couldn't bear to think that she would be consumed by guilt about what they had done if she did decide to go back to Tim.

'I know we crossed a lot of boundaries to-night, Bella,' he said gruffly, trying to batten down the thought of how he would feel if that happened. 'But there's no need to feel…well, *awkward* about what's happened. We've always been friends and I hope that we can still be friends from now on too.'

'If that's what you want.'

Her voice echoed with scepticism and Mac grimaced, understanding completely why she had difficulty believing him. Friends didn't usually make mad passionate love, did they? They definitely didn't cross that boundary! The thought of how hard it was going to be to think of her as a friend after tonight was too much to handle and he shrugged, opting for the easier route, a half-truth.

'It is. I value our friendship, Bella. I always have.' Bending, he dropped what he hoped was a friendly kiss on her cheek, drawing back when he felt his body immediately respond. So much for friendship, he thought wryly as he opened the door. All it took was one chaste little kiss and he was up and running again!

He made his way to the lift, pausing briefly to wave before he stepped inside. He heard the apartment door close as the lift set off and sighed. If only that was the end of the matter, but there was no point kidding himself:

tonight was going to have far-reaching consequences for both of them. He and Bella had slept together and even if they ignored what had happened, it wouldn't go away. It would be like the proverbial elephant in the room whenever they were together, always there but never acknowledged.

He groaned. What in heaven's name had he done?

CHAPTER SEVEN

THE DAYS FLEW PAST. With the schools breaking up for the long summer holiday, there were a lot of visitors in the area and that meant they were busier than ever in the paediatric A&E unit. Bella started early and finished late but she didn't complain. It was easier when she was working. It was when she was on her own that it became a problem. With nothing to distract her, her mind kept returning to what had happened that night in her apartment. She and Mac had made love and whilst she knew that a lot of women would have taken it in their stride, she couldn't do that. That night had been a turning point for her. She had not only discovered how it felt to be a real woman but she had also realised how inadequately suited she was to the role. It was much easier not to have to think about it.

It was a Saturday evening, three weeks after that fateful night, when Bella found herself working with Mac. Up till then their paths had crossed only fleetingly; if she'd been working days, he had been working nights. However, that night they were both rostered to work and she knew that she would have to deal with it. He was already there when she arrived, standing by the desk, laughing at something Laura Watson was saying to him. Bella felt her heart jolt as the memories came flooding back. Mac had looked like that when they had made love. His expression had been softened then by pleasure. If she lived to be a hundred, she would never forget that night, no matter how hard she tried.

He suddenly glanced round and she took a steadying breath as his gaze landed on her. Although neither of them had said anything, they were both aware of the rules. If they were to continue behaving as friends then there must be no harking back to what had happened. They must focus on the here and now, not on what they had done that night.

'It sounds as though you two are having fun,' she said lightly, going over to the desk to sign in.

'Laura was just telling me about one of the children she saw this morning,' Mac explained. He stepped back, ostensibly to give Bella some room, although she suspected that in reality he was trying to avoid touching her. A spurt of anger suddenly shot through her. He had been more than eager to touch her that night, hadn't he?

'Oh, yes?' She smiled up at him, her green eyes holding a hint of challenge. Maybe they had agreed to behave as though nothing had happened, but it wasn't true. They had made love and not once either, but twice. Whether he liked the idea or not, he couldn't just ignore what they had done. 'So what happened?'

'Oh, nothing much. The kid just got a bit confused, that's all.' He glanced round when the phone rang. 'I'll get that.'

He headed to the phone, leaving Bella seething even though she wasn't sure why exactly. After all, it made far more sense to pretend that nothing had happened, especially when there was no chance of there being a repeat. She snorted in disgust as the thought slid into her head. There definitely wasn't going to be a repeat. One night in Mac's arms had caused enough upheaval in her life!

Bella worked her way through the list. There was nothing really serious, just a lot of cuts and bruises, as could be expected when so many children were on holiday. She patched up several cut knees and sent a couple of youngsters for X-rays, and that was it. By the time she was due to take her break, there was just one child waiting to be seen. Mac had finished with his patient and arrived at the desk at the same time as her. He shrugged as he reached over and picked up the last file.

'I'll take this if you want to go for your break, Bella. We may as well make the most of it while it's quiet.'

'Fine.'

Bella headed for the lift. Although she wasn't hungry, a cup of tea would be very welcome. Mac had taken his patient to the cubicles and the waiting room was empty. She was about to step into the lift when the main doors opened and a couple of police officers came in. The female officer was carrying a baby in her arms and Bella paused, wondering what was going on. When Janet, their receptionist, beckoned to her, she hurried over to them.

'What's happened?'

'We received a report to say that a baby had

been left at home on its own,' the male officer explained. 'When we got to the flat, we
found the front door open. The child was inside, screaming its head off. It doesn't appear
to be injured, from what we can tell, but we
need you to check it over, just to make sure.'

'Of course.' Bella led the way to the treatment room. 'If you can put the baby on the
bed, I'll examine it.'

She undid the poppers down the front of
the child's sleepsuit and slipped it off then removed its vest and nappy. It was a little girl
and she appeared to be both clean and well-
nourished. Bella carefully checked her over
and shook her head.

'No, there's nothing wrong with her. She's a
little bit dehydrated but that can soon be sorted
out once we give her a drink. Do you know
where the mother is?'

'No idea. The neighbour who phoned in the
report wasn't able to tell us very much.' The

officer sighed. 'Apparently, she's little more than a kid herself, from what we can gather. We've been on to Social Services and we're hoping they might be able to help us.'

'Do you know her name?' Bella asked slowly, although she had a feeling that she already knew the name of the baby's mother.

'Yes. The neighbour was able to tell us that much at least.' The officer consulted his note-book. 'Freya Watson. We're trying to find out if she's local. If we can trace her family then they might know where she's gone.'

'I can give you their address.' Bella brought up Freya's file on the computer. She gave the policeman the Watsons' address then quickly explained the situation. 'I'd like to think that Freya's parents know where she is, but they were furious when they found out about the baby and refused to have anything more to do with her,' she concluded. 'If Freya has been liv-ing in the flat on her own with the baby then it doesn't look as though they've had a change of heart, does it?'

'No. It doesn't.' The policeman sighed as he wrote everything down in his notebook. 'Right, then. It might turn out to be a waste of time but I'll get on to the station and ask them to send someone round to speak to the girl's parents. The sooner we find out what's happened to her, the better.'

Both officers went outside to make the call, leaving Bella alone with the baby. She sighed as she picked her up and cradled her in her arms. It was no wonder that Freya had found it difficult to cope. Caring for a child on your own was a lot for any woman to deal with. Why, even she would find it hard and she was a lot older than Freya and had far more resources at her disposal. Quite frankly, she couldn't imagine how she would cope if she found herself in the position of being a single parent, not that it was likely to happen. Mac had taken great care to ensure she didn't get pregnant that night they had made love.

A tiny ache awoke in her heart, even though she knew how stupid it was. However, his determination to make sure that there were no consequences from their night of passion simply proved how he really felt about her. Maybe he'd been keen enough to sleep with her but he certainly wasn't looking for anything more.

Mac was surprised to see the police there when he got back from attending to his patient. He went over to the reception desk and asked Janet what was going on.

'They brought in a baby that had been left home alone.' She lowered her voice. 'From what I overheard just now, they seem to think it's Freya Watson's baby.'

'Really?' Mac exclaimed.

He glanced round when he heard footsteps, feeling a whole raft of emotions hit him when he saw Bella walking towards him, carrying the baby in her arms. He had never really thought about having children. Although he liked kids, the fact that he had always avoided commitment meant that it had never been an issue before. Now, however, as he looked at Bella holding the baby, he realised all of a sudden what he was missing.

He could picture it now, imagine how wonderful it would be to have a child of his own, a son or a daughter to love and cherish. His vision blurred as the image inside his head grew stronger. He could see a chubby little baby laughing up at him from its mother's arms now. It was only when the mother's face started to become clearer that Mac realised what was happening and groaned. Picturing Bella as the mother of his children was something he mustn't do! It was a mistake of gigantic proportions to allow himself that much licence. Maybe Bella would have children one day, but one thing was certain: their father would be someone very different from him, a man who came from a background similar to her own.

Bella was relieved when her shift finally ended. It had been a stressful night for so many reasons. The police were still searching for Freya Watson and it was obvious that they were becoming increasingly concerned as time passed and they failed to find any trace of her. The baby had been placed with a foster carer so at least she had the comfort of knowing that the infant was being looked after. However, as she left the hospital, she couldn't shake off the feeling of gloom that weighed her down.

Tim had only wanted to have a child with her to stop her divorcing him—he'd certainly not wanted one before then. And Mac had been at pains to ensure that nothing untoward happened in that department either. Even though she couldn't blame him for behaving responsibly, she couldn't rid herself of the thought that her inability to get in touch with her emotions had a huge bearing on the way both men had acted. The future had never seemed bleaker than it did right then and she realised that there was no point going home as she would never be able to sleep with all these thoughts whizzing around her head.

She left the hospital and headed to a supermarket on the outskirts of town that should open shortly. She hadn't done any food shopping for several weeks and the cupboards were bare. She filled a trolley then paid for her shopping and loaded everything in to her car. At least it had helped to distract her but, as she set off home, she found the same thought churning round and round inside her head: unless she got in touch with her emotions she would never be truly happy.

Maybe it was the stress, but somehow she

must have taken a wrong turning because she found herself on a road she had never driven along before. She drove on for a few more miles, searching for any clues as to where she was. The car's satellite navigation system wasn't any help; it just showed an unmarked road and nothing else. When the road suddenly petered out into a track, Bella decided to turn round rather than risk going any further and getting completely lost. She carefully manoeuvred the car, shunting it backwards and forwards across the narrow track. She had almost completed the turn when there was an almighty bang from the rear of the vehicle.

She got out, her heart sinking when she discovered that one of the back wheels had hit a boulder and had buckled under the impact. There was no way that she could change the wheel herself, but maybe there was a farm up ahead and people who would help her?

Lifting her bag out of the car, she started

walking. Although it was almost the middle of the morning, heavy black clouds hung overhead, obscuring the tops of the surrounding mountains, and she shivered. Although she was wearing a jacket, it wouldn't be much use if it started to rain.

She must have walked a couple of miles before she decided to give up. There had been no sign of a farmhouse and it seemed pointless carrying on. She turned back, grimacing when she felt the first drops of rain start to fall. Within seconds, it was pouring down, sheets of water falling from the sky and soaking through her clothing. Bella walked as fast as she could but the increasingly slippery ground hampered her progress and it took her twice as long to get back to the car.

She climbed in, shivering violently as she started the engine and switched on the heater. Digging in to her bag, she found her mobile phone, intending to call the local garage and ask them to come out and fetch her. It was only when she saw the phone's blank screen that she realised the battery was flat. Tipping back her head, she groaned. What a perfect end to a miserable night!

Mac couldn't shake off the feeling that there was something wrong with Bella. Oh, he understood that it must have been a strain for her to work with him—heaven knew he hadn't found it easy, either. Nevertheless, he couldn't rid himself of the nagging thought that there was something else troubling her. As he left the hospital, he knew that he wouldn't rest until he found out what was the matter, even though he doubted Bella would appreciate his concern. If last night was anything to go by, she would much prefer it if he steered well clear of her!

He drove into town, drawing up in front of the apartment block where she lived. There was no sign of her car in the courtyard and he frowned. He had assumed that she would go straight home after working all night but maybe she had stopped off along the way. He decided to wait but when she still hadn't appeared an hour later, he realised that he might as well give up. There was no point in him hanging around if she had gone off somewhere. He would just have to try again later.

Mac headed home and went straight to bed but, even though he was tired after the busy night, he couldn't sleep. His mind kept churning over all the reasons why Bella might be upset. The fact that Freya had gone missing was bound to have upset her, but was it really that which was troubling her or something of a more personal nature? Try as he might, he couldn't come up with an answer and it was frustrating, to say the least, not to be able to find an explanation.

In the end he gave up any attempt to sleep and got up. He made himself a cup of coffee and stood on the deck while he drank it. It had started to rain but he barely noticed. Was it something he had said? Or was he deluding himself by thinking that anything *he* did could affect her?

He sighed. The truth was that he had no idea how Bella really felt about him. Maybe he should be glad that she seemed to have put what had happened that night behind her, but in his heart he knew it wasn't relief he felt. It was something far more disturbing, an emotion he shouldn't allow himself to feel. To wish that Bella would never forget that night, as he would never forget it, was selfish in the extreme.

Bella trudged on. Although the rain had eased off, it hadn't stopped and cold little flurries of raindrops stung her face as she made her way back along the track. She had decided to walk back to the main road and try to flag down a car in the hope that she could beg a lift into town. However, she hadn't realised just how far she must have driven. At this rate it would be midnight before she reached the road!

Spurred on by the thought, she quickened her pace then had to slow down again when she came to a section where the hillside had caved in. Mud and boulders had been washed down by the rain and covered the track. Bella carefully made her way around the obstruction, pausing when she heard a cry coming from somewhere to her left. She looked around, trying to determine where it had come from, and gasped when she spotted a woman huddled against some bushes. She hurried towards her, her feet slipping this way and that on the muddy ground. It was only as she got closer that she realised it was Freya Watson.

'Freya! What are you doing out here?' she demanded, crouching down beside her.

'I've hurt my ankle,' the girl told her. She ran

a grimy hand over her face and Bella's heart went out to her when she realised that she was crying.

'It's OK,' she said, putting her arm around the girl's shoulders. 'We'll get it sorted out so don't worry. Here, let me take a look.'

She eased up the leg of Freya's jeans, hiding her grimace when she saw her ankle. It was very badly bruised and swollen, the flesh black and purple in places. 'Can you wiggle your toes?' she asked, trying to assess if it was broken or badly sprained, not that it made much difference. It must be extremely painful whichever it was.

'No. I can't move them. Is it broken, do you think?' Freya asked miserably.

'It looks like it.' Bella unwound her scarf from around her neck. 'I'm going to use this as a temporary support. I'll be as gentle as I can but it might hurt a bit.'

Leaving the girl's shoe and sock on, she carefully wound the scarf in a figure of eight fashion around Freya's foot and ankle. 'That should help,' she said after she had finished. 'How did it happen, though? And what were you doing out here in the first place?'

'I was hiding from a man who gave me a lift,' Freya told her. She bit her lip, looking for all the world like a child who knew she had done something wrong.

Bella sighed. 'I think you'd better start from the beginning. But, before you do, have you a mobile phone I can use to call the mountain rescue services? My battery's flat.'

'No. My dad used to pay for my phone but he stopped it after I had Ava and I can't afford to pay for it myself.'

'Don't worry. We'll work something out,' Bella told her, wondering what sort of parents could treat their child the way the Watsons were doing. She would never do that to *her* child, she thought angrily, then sighed when it struck her that it was highly unlikely that she would ever be in the position of having a child of her own.

'So what happened, sweetheart?' she asked, trying not to think about how bleak the future seemed. 'I know you walked out of your flat because the police brought Ava into the hospital to be checked over. She's fine,' she said hastily when she saw the fear in Freya's eyes. 'She's with a foster carer at the moment so she's being well looked after. But what made you leave her in the first place?'

'She wouldn't stop crying,' Freya explained. Tears began to stream down her face once more. 'I tried everything I could think of, too. I fed her and changed her, rocked her and sang to her, but she wouldn't stop. I know I shouldn't have left her on her own but I just couldn't stand it any longer.'

'It must be hard when you don't have anyone to help you,' Bella said gently. 'I take it from what you just told me that your parents haven't had a change of heart?'

'No. They won't even speak to me when I try phoning them.' Freya dried her eyes with the back of her hand. 'I know I was stupid, but it's not as though I've *murdered* someone or anything like that!'

Bella wholeheartedly agreed although she didn't say so. To her mind, the Watsons had behaved deplorably. 'So what happened after you left your flat?'

'I got on a bus. I've no idea where it was going 'cos it really didn't matter. I just needed to get away, you see. The trouble was that when I tried to catch a bus back home, it was after midnight and they'd stopped running.' Freya sighed. 'I started walking when this car drew up and the driver offered me a lift.'

'And you accepted?' Bella asked, her heart sinking at the thought of Freya getting into a stranger's car.

'Yes. He said he'd drive me home but he brought me here instead.' Freya's eyes welled with tears again. 'I was so scared! I managed to jump out of the car when he stopped and hid until he had left. It was pitch-dark and I had no idea where I was so I just stayed here until the morning. I was making my way back to the road when I slipped and hurt my ankle. If you hadn't come along then, I don't know what I'd have done,' she added tearfully.

'Well, I did come so let's not think about that,' Bella said rousingly. She stood up. 'Now, we need to get you back to the main road. Do you think you can hop if I support you? It's either that or leave you here while I go for help.'

'Oh, don't leave me!' Freya exclaimed, obviously terrified by the thought of being left on her own once again.

Bella looped the girl's arm across her shoulders as she helped her to stand up. It wasn't going to be easy to get Freya back to the road, but what choice did she have? Nobody knew they were here and nobody would come looking for them either. Just for a second the thought that Mac might notice her absence crossed her mind before she dismissed it. Mac wouldn't miss her, as he had made it abundantly clear.

CHAPTER EIGHT

MAC WAS GROWING increasingly concerned. He had tried phoning Bella several times but she hadn't responded. He would have put it down to the fact that she didn't want to speak to him, only it appeared that her mobile phone had been switched off. It seemed odd to him, bearing in mind how conscientious she was. How would work contact her in case of an emergency if her phone was switched off?

In the end he went back to her apartment. Although there was still no sign of her car, he rang the bell anyway. There was always a chance that her car had broken down and she had made her way home by some other means. However, after half a dozen rings on the bell, he gave up. She obviously wasn't here, so where was she?

He stood there, trying to think where she might have gone. He knew for a fact that she had made very few friends since she had moved to Dalverston. Although she was well regarded by their colleagues, the fact that she kept herself to herself didn't encourage close friendships—he definitely couldn't picture her dropping in to someone's house for coffee and a chat! No, what friends she did have were all in London, so was it possible that she had driven down there?

It seemed unlikely but it was the only lead he had. He phoned half a dozen mutual friends but drew a blank. Nobody had seen or heard from Bella in months, it seemed. That left him with just one other option, the least appealing one too. He dialled Tim's number, filled with such a mixture of emotions that it was difficult to speak when Tim answered. He had come to Dalverston, sure in his own mind that Bella had been responsible for the demise of her marriage. However, he no longer believed that and it was hard to behave with equanimity as he asked Tim if he had heard from her. He had been wrong to blame her—so very, very wrong. If he lived to be a hundred he would always regret it.

Once again Mac drew a blank. Tim hadn't heard from Bella either, apparently. Mac cut him off, knowing that he would lose it completely if he had to listen to Tim blackening her name again. Although she hadn't gone into any detail about Tim's affair—she'd not had time!—he believed her. And the thought filled him with all sorts of uncharitable feelings towards his former friend. Tim had deliberately lied to him and he wasn't sure if he would ever be able to forgive him for that.

He went back to his motorbike, his face set

as he revved up the engine. He was going to find Bella even if it took him all day!

Progress was excruciatingly slow. They had to stop every few minutes while Freya rested. Bella glanced at her watch, sighing as she realised how much time had passed. They'd barely travelled half a mile and it was already gone midday. She helped Freya sit down in the lee of a large rock and sat down beside her while she tried to decide what to do. It had started to rain again, which would only exacerbate the problem. With the ground becoming increasingly slippery there was a very real danger that Freya might fall again. Bella came to a swift decision, prompted by necessity.

'Look, Freya, this isn't working. I know you don't like the idea of being left on your own but I need to fetch help.' She patted Freya's hand when she started to cry, feeling terrible about abandoning her. However, she would be much faster on her own. 'I'm going to leave you here while I go back to the main road. There's bound to be a car coming along it and I'll flag it down and get them to phone the mountain rescue people. Once they receive the call, it won't be long before we're out of here.'

'You will come back for me?' Freya asked anxiously. She looked round and shuddered. 'What if you can't remember where I am? I mean, it all looks the same to me!'

'I'll use my blouse as a marker.' Bella hurriedly undid her jacket and stripped off her blouse. Rooting around on the ground, she found a sturdy branch and knotted the blouse's sleeves around it. 'Look, I'll push the end of the branch into this crevice in the rock—it will act as a marker so that we'll be able to find you.'

'I suppose so,' Freya agreed reluctantly, obviously unsure about what she was proposing.

'It will be fine, Freya. I promise you.'

Bella gave her a hug then hurried away before *she* started doubting the feasibility of her plan. She had to leave Freya here, otherwise they could be stuck out in the open all day long. The thought spurred her on and she made rapid progress, although it still took her over an hour to reach the main road. She stood at the side of the carriageway, praying that a car would come along soon. She was cold and wet and unutterably weary and all she wanted was to go home and have a long hot bath then climb into bed. Just for a second the image of Mac lying beside her popped into her head before she drove it away. Mac wouldn't be sharing her bed today or in the foreseeable future!

Mac drove all around the town but he still couldn't find any sign of Bella. He tried to imagine where she might have gone but his mind was blank. He sighed as he pulled up outside a coffee shop. Maybe a shot of caffeine would help restore some life to his flagging brain cells. He went in and ordered a triple espresso to go. He added a couple of sachets of sugar to the brew to give it an extra kick then left, stopping when he came face to face with Helen Robertson, their F1 student. She grimaced as she studied the concoction he was nursing.

'You're obviously in need of some serious stimulation if you're thinking of drinking that. It looks lethal to me.'

'Hmm, it probably is. But needs must, and my brain definitely needs a major pick-me-up,' Mac replied with a grimace as he gulped down the coffee.

'It must have been a rough night,' Helen observed, laughing. 'I saw Bella at the supermarket earlier and she looked really washed out.'

'You saw her!' Mac exclaimed. He grabbed hold of Helen's arm. 'When was this?'

'First thing this morning,' Helen told him, looking startled. She glanced over at a young man who was obviously waiting for her and shrugged. 'David and I had been out at a club all night and we popped into the supermarket for some breakfast on our way home. We saw Bella at the checkout, although I don't think she saw us.'

'Thank you so much!' Mac impulsively hugged her. He let her go and grinned. 'I've been worried sick because she wasn't at her apartment or answering her phone. At least I have some idea where she went now.'

'Probably needed to stock up, from the amount of shopping she had,' Helen said lightly.

'Probably,' he agreed.

He said his goodbyes and hurried over to his motorbike. Climbing astride it, he headed out of town to the supermarket, mentally crossing his fingers that he would find Bella there. He sighed. And if he didn't find her, then what? He could hardly report her missing and call out a search party on such flimsy evidence, could he? After all, there was no proof that anything had happened to her—nothing, apart from this gut feeling he had.

He snorted in disgust. Try explaining that to the authorities. They would think he was deranged!

It must have been half an hour before a car finally appeared. Bella stepped into the middle of the road and flagged it down. There was an elderly couple inside and she could see how nervous they looked as she approached the driver's window. Bending down, she smiled reassuringly at them.

'Thank you for stopping. Do you have a mobile phone I can use to call the mountain rescue service? There's been an accident, you see—a young girl has been injured and she needs help.'

The man quickly gave her his phone. Bella made the call, checking with the driver as to their location. Fortunately, he was a local man and he was able to explain exactly where they were. Bella thanked him as she handed back the phone. When the couple asked her if she would like to sit in the car while they waited for the mountain rescue team to arrive, she gratefully accepted. It would be wonderful to get out of the rain even for a short time.

The first of the rescue vehicles arrived just fifteen minutes later and was quickly followed by several others. In a very short time, Bella was leading the team back to where she had left Freya. Thankfully, her makeshift marker had survived the wind and the rain and proved a big help in locating her. Once Freya was loaded onto the stretcher, they headed back. Bella was exhausted by then and finding it difficult to keep up. Relief overwhelmed her when she saw the road up ahead. Just a few more minutes and that would be it, she thought. It was only when she spotted the motorbike parked behind the other vehicles and the man standing beside it that her heart began to pound.

What on earth was Mac doing here?

It had been pure chance that Mac had happened upon the scene. After failing to find Bella at the supermarket, he had driven around, trying to decide what to do next. Although reporting her missing might have seemed premature, that gut feeling he had that something was wrong was growing stronger by the minute. When he came across the mountain rescue vehicles parked beside the road, he could hardly contain his fear. He just *knew* that Bella was involved!

He climbed off the bike, his legs trembling as he went over to speak to one of the team.

He was just about to ask the man if he knew the name of the casualty when a shout went up and he turned to see the rest of the group walking towards them. His heart started to pound when he saw the figure lying on the stretcher. Was it Bella? Was she badly injured? All of a sudden the strength came flooding back to his limbs and he raced towards them. It was only as he drew closer that he realised it wasn't Bella on the stretcher but Freya Watson and he didn't know whether to feel relieved or terrified. Where on earth was she?

'Mac? What are you doing here?'

The sound of her voice had him spinning round. Mac just had a second to take in the fact that she was right there in front of him before instinct took over. Dragging her into his arms, he held her to him, held her as though he would never let her go again. Maybe he wouldn't, he thought giddily. Maybe he would follow his heart and not allow his fear of being rejected, of being left, to ruin things. If he could find the courage to believe in her, to believe in *them*, he could have everything he wanted: Bella in his arms and in his life for ever more.

The next hour passed in a blur. Although Bella did everything that was expected of her, her mind was far removed from what was happening. She kept thinking about the expression on Mac's face, about the way he had held her so tightly, so desperately, and it didn't make any sense. He had behaved as though he truly cared about her but that couldn't be true…

Could it?

The question nagged away at her as she and Freya were ferried to hospital in one of the rescue vehicles. They were taken straight to A&E, where they were met by the senior registrar. Bella quickly explained what had happened, nodding when he immediately decided to send Freya down to X-ray. Once they knew for certain if Freya's ankle was fractured, he could decide on the appropriate course of treatment.

After Freya left, Bella reluctantly agreed to be checked over as well. Although she was sure she was fine, there were procedures to follow and it would be wrong to create a fuss. As expected, she was given a clean bill of health and told that she could leave whenever she wanted. And that was when the tricky bit started. As she exited the cubicle and saw Mac sitting in the waiting room, she had no idea what to do. Had she correctly interpreted his reaction as rather more than relief for the safe deliverance of a friend?

Bella's heart began to race as that thought unlocked the door to several others. Did she want him to feel more than friendship for her, maybe even love? But if he did then how could *she* be sure that she wouldn't ruin things and that her inability to show her true feelings wouldn't destroy whatever he felt? Pain shot through her. Quite frankly, she didn't think she could bear knowing that yet again she had failed as a woman.

Mac could feel the tension building inside him as he waited for Bella to return. He knew that his behaviour must have aroused her suspicions and he was honest enough to admit that the thought scared him too. However, if he intended to win her then he couldn't back down. He had to fight for her. Tooth and claw!

'They said I could go home whenever I liked.'

He started when he realised that she was standing in front of him. He shot to his feet, almost overturning the chair in his haste. 'No damage done, then?' he said and winced at the sheer inanity of the comment.

'No, I'm fine.'

She gave him a quick smile and headed for the door. Mac followed her, pausing when he realised that it was still raining outside. Bearing in mind the soaking she'd had already that day, it seemed decidedly off to drive her home on the back of his motorbike.

'I'll phone for a cab,' he said, hunting his mobile phone out of his jacket pocket.

'What's wrong with your bike?' she asked, one brow arching in a way that made all sorts of complicated things start to happen inside him.

'Oh, ahem, nothing,' he murmured, trying to wrestle his libido back into its box. 'I just thought you'd prefer not to get drenched again.'

'I don't think it matters. I'm soaked as it is, so a drop more rain isn't going to make much difference.'

She gave a little shrug, her breasts rising and falling beneath the clinging folds of her wet jacket, and Mac's libido won the battle, hands down.

'Oh, well, if you're sure, then.'

Mac didn't give her chance to reply as he led

the way to where he had left his motorbike. Quite frankly, he couldn't believe how crassly he was behaving. Usually, it took more than the lift of a brow or the wiggle of a woman's breast to arouse him. He groaned as he took the spare helmet out of the box beneath the seat. Who was he kidding? Bella only had to look at him and he was putty in her hands!

He helped her on with the helmet then swung his leg over the bike, tensing when she settled herself behind him on the seat. He could feel her body pressing against the length of his back and sent up a silent prayer that he would manage to hold out. There must be no stopping along the way, he told himself sternly. And absolutely no thoughts of pulling into a secluded lay-by. He wasn't a teenager but a mature adult who had given up such behaviour years ago. No, he would drive Bella home, make sure she was safely inside her apartment and leave...

'Can we go back to the boat?'

Mac jumped when she leant forward and spoke directly into his ear. He could feel the warmth of her breath on his skin and shuddered. It took every scrap of willpower he could muster not to respond as he yearned to do. 'You don't want to go home to your apartment?' he said hoarsely.

'No. I…well, I would prefer to go to the boat, if you don't mind.'

There was something in her voice that made his skin prickle. Mac nodded, not trusting himself to speak. He drove out of the car park, trying to get a grip, but it was impossible. How could he behave calmly when every instinct was telling him that the reason Bella wanted to go back to the boat was because she wanted to be with *him*?

As he followed the familiar route, he could feel his tension mounting, could feel all sorts of things happening which he had steadfastly avoided in the past. He had refused to allow himself to fall in love before—completely and totally rejected the idea, in fact. He had witnessed his father's devastation when his mother had walked out on them and he had sworn that love wasn't for him; but not any more. Not now that Bella was in his life.

His breath caught as he was forced to confront the truth. How could he *not* fall in love with her when he wanted her so desperately?

Bella took a deep breath as she stepped down from the motorbike. Had she been mad to ask Mac to bring her here? Oh, she knew what was going to happen—there was no use pretending that she didn't. She and Mac would make love again because it was what they both wanted. But surely that would only complicate matters even more?

'Come on. Let's get you inside before you're completely waterlogged.'

Mac placed his hand at the small of her back

to urge her onto the boat and she shivered. Just the feel of his fingers pressing against her flesh made her senses reel. She stepped on board, waiting while he unlocked the cabin door. He turned to her and she could see the uncertainty in his eyes even though he smiled. Did he have doubts about the wisdom of what they were doing too? she wondered. And knew it was true. He was no surer about this than she was.

'Take care on the steps,' he advised her. 'They can be a bit slippery when it rains.'

Bella nodded as she made her way inside the cabin, feeling her nervousness crank itself up another notch or ten. The fact that Mac had doubts only seemed to heighten her own misgivings so that all of a sudden she found herself wishing that she had never suggested coming back here. She should have gone straight home to her apartment, chosen the sensible option rather than placed herself in this position. If they made love again it would be that much harder to do the right thing. No matter how she felt about Mac, she wouldn't *coerce* him into having a relationship with her. It wouldn't be fair. Mac needed a woman who didn't have all these hang-ups. A woman who understood her own feelings and was able to show them too. What he didn't need was someone like her.

The thought was more than she could bear. Bella knew that she had to leave before anything happened. She spun round so fast that she cannoned right into Mac as he stepped down from the last tread. There was a moment when they both froze, when it felt as though time itself had stood still, and then the next second he was hauling her into his arms.

'I was so scared when I couldn't find you!'

His voice grated with fear and a host of other emotions, and she shuddered. It was hard to believe that she had made him feel all those things. Her eyes rose to his and she knew that he could see how she felt—how shocked, how amazed, how overjoyed.

'I didn't think anyone would notice I was missing,' she said truthfully.

'Well, I did!' He rested his forehead against hers and she felt the tremor that passed through him and was shocked all over again.

She had never believed that she was capable of arousing such strong emotions in another person. She had always been so diffident in her approach to life that she had honestly thought it was beyond her, but maybe she had been mistaken. Maybe her experiences with Tim weren't the yardstick by which she should measure any future relationship? The thought made her head reel even more because it opened up so many possibilities that she had thought were denied to her. If she could make Mac feel this way then perhaps there was a future for them after all?

When he bent and kissed her, Bella didn't

hesitate. She simply kissed him back, wanting him to know just how much she needed him. When he murmured something deep in his throat, her heart overflowed with joy. That he wanted her too was blatantly obvious. Swinging her up into his arms, he carried her into the tiny bedroom and laid her down on the bed and she shuddered when she saw the desire burning in his eyes.

'I want to make love to you, Bella, but only if it's what you want as well.'

'It is.' She held out her hand. 'It's what I want, Mac. More than anything.'

He didn't say a word as he took hold of her hand and raised it to his lips, but he didn't need to. The expression on his face said everything that she wanted to hear. Bella could feel herself trembling as he lay down beside her and drew her into his arms. No one had ever looked at her like this before. Looked at her as though she held the key to their future. In that second she knew that, no matter what happened, she would make sure that he didn't get hurt. She loved him so much—far too much to risk his happiness. Maybe she always had loved him too, she thought as she closed her eyes and let their passion sweep her away. She had just been too afraid to admit it before.

They made love with a voracious hunger that had them both trembling. Every kiss, each caress only seemed to fuel their desire for one another. Mac's whole being was consumed by the need to be inside her, but somehow he managed to hold back. He wanted this to be as amazing for Bella as it was for him.

'Mac, *please*!'

The desperation in her voice tipped him over the edge and he entered her with one powerful thrust. He couldn't have held back then even if he'd tried but he didn't need to. Bella was with him every step of the way, her body arching under his as he drove them both to the heights of passion and beyond. They were both shaking when they came back down to earth, both stunned by the sheer intensity of what had happened. Mac knew that he had visited a place he had never been before and that he would never visit again without Bella. It was only with Bella that he could experience such rapture, such a feeling of completeness. Only Bella whom he loved.

The need to tell her how he felt was very strong but something stopped him, a tiny vestige of that fear of rejection that had blighted his life for so long. Although he hated himself for being such a coward, he knew that he needed to come to terms with how he felt before he could take the next step.

Rolling onto his side, he smiled into her eyes, loving the way her face lit up when she smiled back at him. If that weren't proof that she felt something for him, he thought, then what was?

'Now that I've had my wicked way with you,

Dr English, I suppose I'd better feed you,' he said, battening down that delicious thought. Maybe she *did* care about him but he had to be sure—one hundred per cent *sure*—before he went any further. 'How about bacon and eggs—would that hit the spot?'

'Mmm, lovely.' She batted her eyelashes at him. 'I don't suppose you offer your guests breakfast in bed, do you? I'm feeling far too relaxed and comfortable to get up.'

'I suppose I could stretch a point just this once.' He huffed out a sigh, playing up the role of martyr to the full. 'I must warn you, though, that I don't plan to provide such luxuries on a regular basis.'

'Oh, so there are going to be other occasions like this, are there?'

She grinned up at him, her green eyes filled with laughter, and Mac couldn't resist. Bending, he dropped a kiss on her lips, feeling his body immediately stir. Catching hold of her around the waist, he lifted her on top of him.

'I think so. In fact, I'd go so far as to say that I *know* there will.'

He ran his hand down her back, feeling her tremble as her hips were brought into intimate contact with his. That she could feel how much he wanted her wasn't in any doubt. He kissed her long and hungrily, not even surprised by the depth of his desire. Even if he made love to her a dozen times a day, he would still want her, he thought.

Their lovemaking was just as fulfilling the second time round. Mac had to drag himself out of bed afterwards. He knew that Bella must be hungry and he wanted to feed her and take care of her every need. The thought filled him with tenderness as he dragged on his clothes and went to start preparing their meal. Bella had decided to take a shower and he smiled when he heard the water running. He could get used to sharing his life here on the boat with her. Very easily too.

It was the first time he had ever considered such an arrangement and it shocked him. Although he'd had many girlfriends over the years, he had never lived with any of them. It had seemed like a step too far and yet he knew without even having to think about it that living with Bella was what he wanted more than anything. He wanted the intimacy that came from living together, wanted to get to know all the little things that made her tick, like her favourite food and which programmes she enjoyed watching on television. His head began to spin because if he went down that route then it was just a small step to the next, but was he ready for that, ready for the ultimate commitment—marriage?

He wished he knew, wished with all his heart that he could simply close his eyes and *know* it was what he wanted but he couldn't. Not yet.

That last pesky remnant of fear was still niggling away at the back of his mind and, until he had rid himself of it, he couldn't make the final decision. He sighed heavily. Please heaven, he prayed he wouldn't leave it too late and end up losing her.

CHAPTER NINE

'I AM ABSOLUTELY STUFFED!'

Bella groaned as she laid down her knife and fork. She had eaten far too much but it had been hard to resist when Mac had placed the meal in front of her. Now she smiled at him, loving the way his eyes lit up as he smiled back—another indication of how he felt about her, perhaps?

'Are you trying to make me fat, Dr Mac-Intyre?' she said, trying not to get too hung up on the idea. Maybe they *had* made love and maybe it *had* been marvellous but she mustn't take anything for granted. 'Because you're definitely going to succeed if you keep cooking me meals like that!'

'From what I can recall, there's no danger of you getting fat.'

He smiled into her eyes and Bella felt a wave of heat flow through her when she realised that he was remembering how she had looked when they had made love. She bit her lip as she was suddenly assailed by the memory of his powerful body. The strange thing was that she had never been aroused by a man's physical appearance in the past. Even as a teenager she hadn't done what most teenage girls did and stuck posters on her wall of the latest male heart-throb. Looks hadn't aroused her and yet the memory of Mac's body, so lean and yet so powerful, made her tremble. Picking up her cup, she buried her face in it, praying that he wouldn't guess what she was thinking. Lusting after him definitely wasn't something a woman of her age should be doing!

'Bella?' His voice was so bone-meltingly gentle that she reacted as though he had actually touched her. Her hand was trembling as she placed the cup on the table and she saw him look at her in concern. Leaning forward, he covered her hand with his. 'You're not upset about what we did, are you, sweetheart?'

'No.' She shook her head to emphasise that she meant what she said. She didn't regret making love with him again, although she couldn't help wondering what was going to happen from here on. Would Mac expect them to be friends who occasionally slept together from now on? She hoped not, even though she wasn't sure exactly what she did want them to be.

'Then what's wrong?' He squeezed her fingers. 'Tell me. I want to know if there's something worrying you.'

'There isn't. I'm fine.'

She smiled brightly back at him, not wanting to admit her fears when she felt so ambivalent. Did she want Mac in her life for ever and ever or simply for the foreseeable future? Oh, she loved him—she was sure about that. But *for ever* was a long time and she had no idea if it was expecting too much to aim for that.

All of a sudden the situation seemed way too complicated. Bella pushed back her chair and started gathering up their plates. She needed time to think, time to work out what she really wanted… Her breath caught as she turned to carry the plates to the sink and saw Mac watching her. She wanted Mac. But did she have the right to want him when she wasn't sure if she could fulfil his needs?

'I think I'll have a shower.' Mac stood up. Picking up their cups, he brought them over to the sink. He put them down on the counter then bent and dropped a kiss on the nape of her neck. Bella shuddered when she felt his lips brush against her skin. It was hard to be sensible and act responsibly when she felt this way!

'Bella.'

Her name on his lips was like a caress. When he turned her into his arms, she didn't hesitate. Maybe she didn't know what was going to happen in the future but she did know what she wanted to happen right now. Lifting her face to his, she kissed him back, her mouth clinging to his as she sought reassurance. Surely this desire they felt for one another could be seen as a good omen?

They made love once again and once again it was unlike anything Mac had experienced before. The feel of Bella's satin-smooth skin gliding beneath his fingertips aroused him as nothing had ever done in the past. He could only marvel at how different it was to make love to her. How special. How totally fulfilling. It wasn't just his senses that were engaged when they made love but his spirit too. It felt as though he had found himself in her arms, discovered the real person beneath the public image. He hadn't realised to what extent he put up a front between himself and the world, but he did now. With Bella he could be himself. Completely and wholly himself. The thought was so poignant that it washed away the last remnants of fear. Framing her face between his hands, he looked deep into her eyes.

'I love you, Bella.' He had to break off at that point because words failed him; only to be expected when it was the first time he had ever uttered them. Not once had he told a woman that he loved her because it wouldn't have been true, but it was true now. He loved Bella with all his heart and with every atom of his being too.

'I...' Bella started to speak and then stopped. Mac could see the shock on her face and understood. It was a momentous occasion for both of them. He laughed softly as he dropped a kiss on the tip of her nose.

'I know. I feel as stunned as you do, my love.

I think we both need a few minutes to get our heads round the idea, don't you?'

He stood up, feeling tenderness engulf him when he saw the expression on her face, a mixture of shock mingled with a growing excitement. Obviously, his announcement hadn't come as an unwelcome surprise then, he thought a shade smugly. As he made his way into the bathroom, Mac could feel happiness bubbling up inside him. Telling Bella how he felt had been a huge gamble, but it appeared to have paid off. Clearly, she had feelings for him too, and now all he needed to do was to persuade her to admit that she loved him back and they could look towards the future.

He grinned as he poured shower gel into his palm and started to lather himself. Maybe he was guilty of putting the cart before the horse, but it looked very much as though he and Bella might be riding off into the sunset. Together!

* * *

Bella washed the dishes and put them away in the cupboard. Mac kept the boat immaculately tidy and she didn't want to leave everywhere in a mess. After all, she would hate to think that he considered her to be a nuisance…

She sat down abruptly on the couch as all the strength suddenly seeped from her limbs. From what Mac had said before, there seemed little danger of that! He had told her that he loved her, but could it be true?

A tremor ran through her as she recalled the expression on his face as he had made the admission. He was either a brilliant actor or he had been telling her the truth and all of a sudden she knew which she wanted it to be. She wanted Mac to be a permanent part of her future!

Her breath caught as her mind raced away with the idea. Being with Mac, day in and day out, would be like a dream come true. He would always be there for her, always support her, always put her first. His loyalty and steadfastness were qualities she had admired ever since they had first met. Even though she had been a little wary of him initially because of the differences in their backgrounds, she had always known that he would be there for her. That was why it had hurt so much when he had blamed her for the failure of her marriage. She had expected him to understand why she'd had to end it and the fact that he hadn't done so had knocked her for six. Did he now accept that she wasn't at fault? she wondered suddenly. She hoped so. If they were to have that glorious future she longed for then they had to trust one another completely.

It was a tiny doubt, like a black mark on an otherwise bright and shiny canvas. Bella knew that she needed to talk to him about it before they went any further. She made a fresh pot of coffee while she waited for him to finish showering, feeling her nervousness increasing by the second. If Mac didn't believe in her innocence then this could be the beginning and the end for them.

'Mmm, coffee.' Mac came into the cabin. He grinned as he came over and caught her around the waist. 'Not only beautiful and sexy, but you can read my mind as well. It's no wonder that I love you, Bella English.'

He kissed her lingeringly, his lips teasing hers until Bella's head reeled. She kissed him back, feeling the tiny niggling doubt disappear. Mac wouldn't feel this way unless he believed in her. And it was the most marvellous feeling in the world to know that his love for her was everything he professed it to be. When he raised his head, she knew that this was the moment she should tell him how she felt too. She loved him and now that all her doubts had been erased, she wanted to make that clear.

'Mac, I...' She got no further when at that

precise moment his phone rang. Mac groaned as he glanced over at where it lay on the table.

'Typical! Why do the wretched things always ring at the most inconvenient times?' Reaching over, he picked it up and she saw his expression change as he glanced at the screen.

'Hello, Tim,' he said flatly. He paused while he listened to what the other man was saying. 'Yes, I found her and she's fine… Of course. She's right here.'

Bella's heart bumped painfully against her ribs as he handed her his phone. She wasn't sure why Mac looked so distant all of a sudden. Surely he didn't think that she was eager to speak to her ex after what had just happened between them?

She was curt almost to the point of rudeness as she told Tim that she had taken a wrong turning on her way back from the supermarket and that was why she had gone missing. She didn't add anything about Freya and what else had happened because she wanted to end the call as quickly as possible.

She glanced at Mac, who had gone to stand by the sink, and felt her heart start racing when she saw how grim he looked. Mac obviously believed that she was pleased to hear from Tim, but nothing could be further from the truth. That part of her life was over and there was no chance of her and Tim getting back together. She realised that she needed to make that clear to Tim, so when he asked if they could meet up, she agreed. She couldn't move forward until she had drawn a line under the past.

'Tim was just calling to check that I was all right,' she said quietly as she ended the call. Mac didn't say anything and she hurried on, wanting to make the situation clear to him as well. 'He wants to see me and I've agreed.'

'So I heard.' Mac's expression held a contempt that chilled her to the core. 'Maybe I should congratulate you. It appears that you two have resolved your differences at last. I hope you will be very happy together.'

'No! It isn't like that,' she began but he didn't let her finish.

'Don't bother explaining. It's obvious that Tim still loves you if he's so eager to talk things through with you. And you obviously still love him if you've agreed to meet him after everything that's happened.' He gave a dismissive shrug that made her heart curl up inside her. 'I'm only glad that I was able to help in some small way. It appears that sleeping with me has helped you realise exactly what you want from life, and it certainly isn't an affair with me.'

Bella couldn't believe what she was hearing. Oh, she understood the words all right—they were plain enough. However, the fact that Mac believed that she had slept with him to help her decide if she should go back to Tim was beyond her comprehension. If he loved her, as he claimed to do, then he would *know* that she was incapable of such behaviour.

All of a sudden she couldn't take any more, couldn't bear to stand there and listen to him accusing her of such terrible deeds. Snatching up her bag, she pushed past him and ran up the steps to the deck. She heard him shouting her name but she didn't stop. What was the point? He had said everything that needed to be said, made it abundantly clear how he felt. Oh, maybe he had thought that he loved her but it wasn't true. It couldn't be when he didn't know in his heart that she would *never* go back to Tim after what they had done. Once again the thought that it was all down to her rose to the surface to taunt her. If she had only shown Mac how she really felt, convinced him that it was *him* she wanted and no one else, told him she loved him too even just once then maybe things would have turned out very differently.

Tears streamed down her face as she ran along the towpath, tears of grief for what she'd had so fleetingly and lost so quickly. It hurt so much, far more than when her marriage had ended, but that was to be expected. This time she had given her heart and had it ripped to shreds and thrown back at her. It had to be the most painful rejection of all.

Mac sank down onto the couch after Bella left. He knew that he should go after her but he felt incapable of doing anything at that moment. Bella was planning to go back to Tim; could it be true? But if it wasn't true then why had she agreed to meet Tim?

His head reeled as question after question assailed him. He realised that he needed to find out the answers before he drove himself mad, and leapt to his feet. There was no sign of Bella when he reached the deck so he set off at a run, expecting to catch up with her in the lane, but there was no sign of her there either. His heart began to thump as he wondered where she had gone. It was only when he caught a glimpse of the bus disappearing around the bend that he had the answer to that question at least. As for all the others, well, he would need to speak to her. She was the only one who knew the truth.

Mac made his way to where he had parked his motorbike. He started the engine, feeling his stomach churning with dread as all his old fears of rejection surged to the forefront. Maybe he did need answers but he could only pray that he was strong enough to hear them.

'Four-year-old in cubicle three—Oscar Starling. Mum thinks he's swallowed some detergent. Who wants it? You or Mac?'

'I'll take it.'

Bella grabbed the child's notes, turning away when she saw Trish look at her in surprise. There was no way that she intended to explain why she was so eager to take the case. Mac had been trying to get her on her own all morning long, but she had no intention of talking to him. That was why she hadn't answered the door when he had turned up at her apartment yesterday after she'd got back from the boat. What was there to say, after all? That she had no intention of going back to Tim? Why should he believe her when she had such difficulty expressing her true feelings?

Bella pushed back the curtain, preferring to focus on her patient's needs rather than her own problems. There was a little boy sitting on the examination couch and he smiled when she went in.

'I've got a new tractor,' he told her importantly, holding up a bright green toy tractor for her to admire.

'You lucky boy. It's beautiful.' Bella took the toy off him and ran it across the couch, making appropriate tractor noises. She handed it back then turned to his mother and smiled. 'Hello, I'm Dr English. I believe Oscar may have swallowed some detergent—is that right?'

'Yes.' Louise Starling sighed. 'He was playing in the kitchen with his tractor. He never normally goes in the cupboard where I keep the detergent but he did today. I'd gone upstairs and when I came down, he had the box on the floor. I use those liquid capsules and one of them was broken open. The liquid in them is bright blue and I could see that Oscar's lips were stained blue as well.'

'I see.' Bella turned to the little boy. 'Did you swallow a lot of mummy's detergent, Oscar?'

He shook his head. 'No, 'cos it tasted funny.' He zoomed the tractor across the couch and grinned at her. 'I spat it out on the floor.'

'Good boy.'

Bella ruffled his hair, thinking how adorable he was. It must be wonderful to have such a bright and happy child. The thought naturally reminded her of her own situation and she swallowed her sigh. There was little chance of her ever having a child when she ended up driving away every man she met. She tried to put the thought out of her mind as she asked Louise Starling if she had brought any of the capsules with her.

'I brought the box.' Louise handed Bella the box of detergent capsules. She grimaced. 'I saw something on TV about taking the container with you if your child swallows something he shouldn't. I remember thinking that it would never happen to Oscar as I'm so careful, but it just goes to show, doesn't it?'

'You mustn't blame yourself,' Bella said sympathetically. 'Even the most careful parents can't always predict what their children are going to do. Right, I'll go and phone the National Poisons Information Service and see what they advise. However, I don't think that you need to worry too much. From what Oscar has told us, he didn't ingest very much of the detergent.'

Bella went to the desk and called the NPIS helpline. They kept a list of household products on file and were able to advise her on the best course of treatment. Fortunately, these particular capsules weren't highly toxic and, because so little of the detergent had been ingested, they agreed that Oscar wasn't in any immediate danger. Bella went back and broke the good news to the little boy's mother then set about treating him, which involved getting him to drink a large tumbler of water. He was as good as gold and drank it all without a murmur, making her smile.

'You are a good boy, Oscar. I want you to drink another glass of water when Mummy takes you home—will you do that for me?'

Oscar nodded, more interested in his tractor than in what was happening. Bella laughed as she lifted him off the couch. 'Come with me and I'll see if I can find you a sticker for being such a good boy.'

He happily held her hand as she led the way from the cubicle. They kept a pile of stickers behind the desk so Bella sorted through them until she found one with a tractor on it. Crouching down, she stuck it onto the child's T-shirt. 'There you go. It says, "I'm a star patient!"—which you are.'

Bella smiled as Oscar excitedly showed the sticker to his mother. She told Louise to bring him back if she was at all worried then sat down to write up the child's notes after they left. It was almost lunchtime and, once she had finished her notes, she would go to the canteen and make herself eat something. She hadn't been able to force down anything except a cup of coffee that morning and she couldn't keep going on that alone. If she was to do her job properly then she needed to look after herself. After all, if she was never going to have that family she had longed for then she would need to focus on her career.

It seemed like a poor substitute even though she loved her job but Bella knew that she had to be realistic. Oh, maybe she did have dreams and maybe it was hard to relinquish them, especially the dreams she'd had about her and Mac and the golden future they would enjoy together, but the longer she clung to her dreams, the more painful it would be. She and Mac had had their chance and it hadn't worked out. The sooner she accepted that, the better.

By the time lunchtime rolled around, Mac was finding it difficult to contain his frustration. Bella had evaded his every attempt to speak to her. Oh, he had tried—tried umpteen times, in fact—but she had managed to avoid him. It was fast reaching the point where the rest of the team were bound to notice that something was going on, but hard luck. It wasn't his doing; it was Bella's. And if people started gossiping about them then she only had herself to blame!

Mac grimaced, aware that he was being very unfair. He had started this by making those accusations. He had spent a sleepless night, thinking about what had happened, and by the time morning arrived he knew that he had been wrong to jump to such hasty conclusions. Bella would never have tried to use him that way— it simply wasn't in her nature. He had allowed his fear of getting hurt to skew his judgement and he owed her an apology, but the big question was: would she accept it? From the way she had behaved towards him that morning, he very much doubted it.

His spirits were at an all-time low as he saw his patient out and returned to the desk. He paused when he spotted Bella sitting at the computer. There was nobody else around so maybe this was the moment he'd been waiting for. The thought of losing her if she went back to Tim was bad enough, but it would be so much worse if they parted on such bad terms. He needed to make his apologies and at least try to salvage something from the situation even if it was all too little. He took a couple of hurried strides then stopped when the emergency telephone rang. It felt as though he was being torn in two. Part of him desperately wanted to ignore the phone and speak to Bella, while another part urged him to respond to the summons.

In the end duty won. Mac snatched up the receiver, listening intently while the operator relayed the details. There'd been an accident at a level crossing on the outskirts of town. A train had hit a car that had stalled on the track and a number of people had been seriously injured, including several children. Mac confirmed that they would send a team and hung up then pressed the call button to summon the rest of the staff. Once everyone had gathered around the desk, he explained what had happened and what they would do.

'Bella, Laura and I will attend the accident as we've all done the major incident training course. That leaves Helen, Trish and Bailey to cover here.' He turned to Janet. 'Can you phone Adam and ask him to come in?' he asked, referring to their consultant, Adam Danvers. 'He was at a finance meeting this morning but it should be over by now so it shouldn't be a problem.'

Once everything was organised, Mac led the way to the room where they kept all their equipment. After they had donned weatherproof suits, they each collected a backpack containing everything they might need, from basic dressings to surgical instruments. It was impossible to foretell what they would have to deal with and they needed to be prepared. A rapid response car was waiting when they exited the building. Bella didn't look at him as she climbed into the back and beckoned to Laura to sit beside her.

Mac's mouth compressed as he slid into the passenger seat. He had missed his chance to try and sort things out with her and, if she had anything to do with it, he wouldn't get another opportunity either. Maybe he should think about cutting short his contract and signing on for the next aid mission? He had planned on staying in England for a while, but it would be better than having to work with Bella if she and Tim got back together. To see her day in and day out, knowing that she didn't love him but someone else, would be unbearably painful. Quite frankly, he doubted if he could handle it.

He closed his eyes as they set off with lights flashing and siren blaring, trying to blot out the thought of the dark and lonely future that lay ahead of him. Without Bella in his life, it felt as though he had very little to look forward to.

CHAPTER TEN

IT WASN'T THE FIRST major incident that Bella had attended but it had to be the most serious. The train was a high-speed express and many of its carriages had been derailed. The fire and rescue crews were working their way along the track, searching for any injured passengers, and by the time they arrived there were over a hundred people gathered at the side of the railway line. It was more than a little daunting to be faced with so many people who needed help, but Mac took it in his stride.

'We need to find out where the children are. It may seem hard-hearted to ignore the adults but there are other teams of medics who can deal with them. Our brief is to concentrate on the kids first and foremost.'

Bella nodded, feeling her initial panic subside in the face of his calmness. 'So what do you want us to do?' she asked, her heart lifting when he smiled at her. She battened it down, knowing how easy it would be to allow herself to think that it meant something. Mac had proved beyond any shadow of a doubt that he didn't really love her and she must never forget that.

'I'll have a word with the officer in charge. Incident control said that there were two children who'd been seriously injured, although there may be others. However, we'll start with them.'

'Fine. Laura and I will go and check on that group over there,' Bella replied dully, confining her thoughts to what was happening. There was no point thinking about how much she loved him when it wouldn't make any difference. Mac may have thought that he loved her; however, the way he'd reacted yesterday proved it wasn't true. If he had loved her, as he'd claimed, then he would have known that she would never go back to Tim!

Her heart felt like lead as she and Laura made their way over to a group of teenagers huddled beside the track. There were three boys and two girls in the party and they all looked deeply shocked. One of the boys had a large gash on his forehead so Bella cleaned it up and applied butterfly stitches to hold the edges together. He would need to go to hospital and have a scan to check that he hadn't suffered a head injury. The rest of the group had suffered only minor cuts and bruises so she told them to wait there until they were told they could go home. They all had mobile phones and they'd called their parents so she guessed it wouldn't be long before they were collected.

As for the aftermath of what they had witnessed, that was something no one could predict. Some would put it behind them and get on with their lives, while others might be permanently affected. It all depended on the type of person they were. Take her, for instance. She had spent her life distancing herself from other people so it was doubly ironic that now she had finally got in touch with her emotions, it was to have them thrown back in her face. It was a sobering thought but thankfully she didn't have time to dwell on it as Mac came over just then and drew her aside.

'The injured children are still on the train. The crew who found them decided it was too risky to try and move them.'

'Sounds bad,' Bella said quietly, her heart sinking. 'Do you know which carriage they're in?'

'One of the crew's going to take us to them.' Mac looked at her. 'Are you OK about this,

Bella? I know how upsetting this kind of situation can be, so say if it's too much for you.'

'I'm fine,' she snapped, determined that she wasn't going to let her newly discovered emotions get the better of her. Mac didn't love her. If she said it often enough then maybe she would believe it and not keep reading too much into everything he said.

'Fair enough.'

He shrugged but she saw the hurt in his eyes and had to bite her tongue to stop herself saying something. He didn't need her reassurances. He didn't need anything at all from her. The thought stayed with her as they followed one of the fire crew along the track. They came to the first two carriages, the ones directly behind the engine, and Bella grimaced. The carriages were lying on their side, in a mangled mess halfway down the embankment, and it was hard to believe that anyone sitting in either of them had survived.

'You're going to need to be extremely careful,' the fireman warned them. 'There's a lot of broken glass and metal in there. We've tried to stabilise the carriages as best we can to stop them sliding any further down the embankment but if we tell you to get out then no arguing—just do it. One of the kids is in the first carriage and the other is in the second, but you'll need to make your way inside through here. A couple of our guys are waiting with them.'

Bella nodded, saving her breath as she set about levering herself up into the carriage. It was a long way and there were very few footholds so it wasn't easy.

'Here. Put your foot in my hands and I'll give you a boost up.'

Mac made a cup with his hands and after a moment's hesitation Bella placed her foot in it. He boosted her up until she could grab hold of the fireman's hand. He hauled her the rest of the way, waiting until Mac joined them before he led them inside. It was strangely disorientating to walk along what was actually the side wall of the carriage, scrambling over seats and tables that had sheared away from their housings. Bella was glad when they reached the first casualty, a young girl, roughly ten years of age.

'You stay with her and I'll check out the other child,' Mac told her as they paused. His eyes darkened. 'Just mind what you're doing, Bella. It's only too easy to have an accident yourself in this kind of situation.'

Bella nodded, unable to speak when her throat felt as dry as a bone. She crouched down and began examining the girl, focusing all her attention on what she was doing. It would be a mistake to read anything into the way Mac had looked at her, she reminded herself sternly. Her heart began to thump because there was no way that she could stop herself. Despite what had happened, she wanted Mac to be concerned about her.

She took a deep breath but the truth had to be faced. She wanted him to feel all *sorts* of things when he looked at her, and especially love.

Mac did his best but the boy's injuries were just too severe. He died a short time later and now all that was left to do was to inform his parents. They had been injured as well and had already been ferried to hospital.

His heart was heavy as he made his way back through the train. Breaking bad news to relatives was always hard and even worse when it concerned a child. He couldn't imagine how people coped with such a tragedy; he knew he'd find it impossibly difficult. If he had a child then he would love it with every fibre of his being, and it was such a poignant thought in the circumstances. Bella was the only woman he had ever wanted to have a child with and it was never going to happen.

It was hard to hide how devastated the thought made him feel as he stopped beside her. She looked up and he had to bite back the words that were clamouring to get out. It wasn't fair to put her under any pressure, to make her feel guilty because she loved Tim and not him. People couldn't choose who they fell in love with, although even if he could have done he would have still chosen Bella. Right from the first moment they had met, he had known in his heart that she was the only woman for him.

It was hard to contain his emotions at that thought but somehow he managed to get them under control. 'Have you nearly finished here?'

'Yes. She's stable and ready to be moved. How about the other child?'

Mac shook his head, feeling tears welling behind his eyelids. He was at emotional overload and it would take very little to make him break down. 'He didn't make it.'

'Oh, I'm so sorry!' Reaching up, she touched his hand, just the lightest, briefest of contacts, but he felt the touch like a brand burning into his skin.

He turned away, terrified that he would do something crazy. He mustn't beg her to stay with him, mustn't try to *coerce* her. She had to want him as much as he wanted her, otherwise there was no point. She would only end up by leaving him and he couldn't bear the thought of that happening... Although could it be any worse than what was happening right now? Could he feel any more devastated than he did at this very moment, knowing that he had lost her?

The questions thundered inside his head as he made his way from the train. He had intended to find the officer in charge and update him about what had happened to the boy. However, he'd only gone a couple of yards when he heard shouting behind him and spun round. His heart seemed to seize up as he watched the wrecked carriages start to slide down the embankment. There was a sickening screech of metal being ripped apart, the sound of glass shattering, and then silence.

Mac stood where he was, unable to move as fear turned his limbs to stone. Bella was trapped somewhere inside that tangle of broken glass and metal!

Bella had been about to stand up when she heard someone shouting and the next second she felt the carriage begin to move. Grabbing hold of a table, she clung on as it gathered momentum, jolting and bouncing its way down the embankment. Bits of broken glass and metal were being flung around and she gasped when a shard of metal cut into her neck. She could feel the warm stickiness of blood pouring from the cut but she was too afraid to let go of her handhold to check it out. Fortunately, Katie, the young girl she'd been treating, was wedged between a couple of overturned seats and they provided some protection for her. However, Bella could see the fear in her eyes and reacted instinctively.

'It's OK, sweetheart. The carriage has just slipped a little but it will stop in a moment.'

Reaching out, she squeezed Katie's hand, praying that she wasn't being overly optimistic. The bank was very steep at this point, falling away to the river at the bottom, and she didn't want to imagine what would happen if it slid all the way down. When they suddenly came to a jarring halt, she was overwhelmed by relief. She gingerly straightened up, holding on to the table when she felt the carriage sway. She could see out of the window now and her heart sank when she realised that the carriages had come to rest against some scrubby-looking trees. It seemed unlikely that they could support their weight for very long.

'We need to get you out of here.' The fireman who had accompanied them onto the train appeared. His expression was grim as he glanced out of the window. 'Those trees won't be able to support this weight for much longer, so we're going to have to move you and the girl straight away.'

'I understand,' Bella said quietly, doing her best to hide her concern for Katie's sake. Crouching down, she concentrated on making sure that the supports she had placed around the girl's hips and legs were securely fastened. Katie had a fractured pelvis plus fractures to both femurs and it was essential that the breaks were stabilised before they attempted to move her. Once Bella was sure that she had done all she could, she stood up. 'Right, there's nothing more I can do. Let's get her out of here.'

The fire crew carefully eased the girl out

from between the seats. They had a stretcher ready and they slid her onto it, passing it from hand to hand as they lifted her over all the debris. Bella followed them, biting her lip against the pain from the cut in her neck. It had stopped bleeding, thankfully, but it was definitely going to need stitching from what she could tell. They reached the door at last and the lead fireman turned to her.

'We'll get you out first. That way, you'll be on hand if she needs anything.' He lowered his voice. 'It won't be easy to get her out of here, so be prepared, Doc.'

Bella nodded, understanding how difficult it was going to be. Not only would the crew need to lift the stretcher up to reach the opening, they would have to raise it at an angle to get it through the gap. She could only pray that the pain relief she had given the girl would be sufficient. In other circumstances, she would have insisted on them waiting while she topped it up but that wasn't an option right now. At any moment, the carriages could start to move again and the consequences of that happening didn't bear thinking about. She allowed one of the crew to boost her up to reach the opening, gasping when she discovered that Mac was there waiting to help her down. He gripped tight hold of her hands and she could see the relief in his eyes.

'Are you all right?' he asked, his deep voice throbbing with an emotion that made her heart start to race.

'I…I think so.'

'Good.'

He squeezed her fingers then quickly lowered her down to the ground where another member of the crew was waiting to escort her to safety. Within seconds Bella found herself at the top of the embankment. She sat down abruptly on the grass as her head began to whirl. Maybe it was the stress of what had happened the previous day allied to the amount of blood she had lost, but all of a sudden she felt incredibly dizzy. Putting her head between her knees, she made herself breathe slowly and deeply but the feeling of faintness simply got worse. As she slid into unconsciousness, the last thing she heard was Mac's frantic voice calling her name.

CHAPTER ELEVEN

MAC WAS ALMOST beside himself with fear by the time he returned to Dalverston General. He would have happily sold his soul to the devil if it had meant he could have gone with Bella in the ambulance that had ferried her and Katie to the hospital, but there'd been no way that he could have left Laura on her own. He'd had to stay, even though it had been the hardest thing he had ever done. Bella was injured and he needed to be with her even if it wasn't what she wanted.

The thought weighed heavily on him as he made his way to A&E. Nick Rogers, one of the senior registrars, was on duty and he grinned when he saw Mac coming in. 'Bit of excitement today, eh? I drew the short straw and had to stay here. Story of my life—I never get the really interesting jobs!'

Mac knew that Nick was joking and that he was as committed to his job as they all were, but he took exception to the comment. 'You wouldn't say that if you'd seen the state of those poor souls who were on the train,' he snapped.

'Sorry.' Nick held up his hands in apology and Mac sighed, aware that he had overreacted.

'No. It's me. Take no notice. Anyway, you've got Bella in here. Can I see her?'

'Sure. She's in cubicle four... No, wait a sec; she's just gone down to radiography.'

'Radiography?' Mac repeated. His heart gave a little jolt as he looked at Nick in horror. 'She's having an X-ray?'

'Yep. That cut on her neck is deep and I

wanted to check there was nothing lodged in it so I've sent her down for an X-ray.'

'I was hoping it would just need stitching,' Mac murmured, his stomach churning sickeningly. If there was something lodged in the cut—a piece of glass or a sliver of metal, perhaps—then Bella might need surgery and he couldn't bear the thought of her having to go through such an ordeal.

'Probably will,' Nick replied cheerfully. 'It's just best to err on the side of caution, as I said.'

'I…er… Yes, of course.'

Mac did his best to pull himself together as he thanked the other man. He knew he was overreacting but he couldn't help it. This was Bella and he simply couldn't take a balanced view where she was concerned. He hurried to the lift, tapping his foot with impatience as it carried him down to the radiography unit. There was nobody in the waiting room so he pressed the bell, his impatience mounting as he waited for someone to answer. When the door to one of the X-ray suites opened, he spun round, his heart leaping when he saw Bella being wheeled out by a porter.

'Mac, what are you doing here?' she exclaimed when she saw him. 'I thought you'd still be at the accident.'

'All the children have been either moved to hospital or sent home,' he explained as he went over to her. 'Nick told me you were here, having an X-ray done on your neck.'

'Yes. Thankfully, there's nothing in it. Once it's stitched up I should be right as rain.'

She dredged up a smile but Mac could see the wariness in her eyes and realised that she wasn't sure what was going to happen. All of a sudden he couldn't stand it any longer, couldn't bear to tiptoe around any more. He loved her! He wanted her! And he wanted her to know that too.

His heart was thumping as he turned to the

porter and told him that he would take Dr English back to A&E. Once the man had disappeared, he pushed Bella to a quiet corner where they wouldn't be disturbed. Crouching down in front of the wheelchair, he looked into her eyes, knowing that he was about to take the biggest gamble of his life. Telling her that he loved her had felt like a huge risk at the time, but it wasn't nearly as massive as this. This was so enormous that it scared him witless and yet it was what he *had* to do if he was to have a chance of achieving what he wanted so desperately—Bella and that happy-ever-after he yearned for.

Capturing her hands, he raised them to his mouth, feeling his panic subside as soon as he felt the warmth of her flesh against his lips. He could do this. He really could! 'I love you, Bella. I know I already told you that but then I went and ruined things by overreacting when

Tim phoned. There's no excuse for what I said. I was wrong and I bitterly regret it.'

'I would never have slept with you just to work out how I feel about Tim,' she said softly.

'I know that.' Mac had to force the words past the lump in his throat when he heard the pain in her voice. He knew that she was telling him the truth and the fact that he had caused her such anguish filled him with guilt. 'I am so sorry, my love. Can you ever forgive me?'

'Yes. If I'm sure that you believe me.' She looked steadily back at him. 'I couldn't cope if you kept on doubting me all the time. I have to know that you believe in me, Mac. Our relationship won't work if you're continually wondering if I'm telling you the truth.'

'I know that.' He sighed as he leant forward and kissed her gently on the mouth. He drew back when he felt his body immediately stir. It was too soon for that. They needed to sort this out before they went any further. *If* they went any further. The thought spurred him on.

'I hate myself for hurting you, Bella. However, the truth is that I've always had a problem about trusting people since I was a child and my mother left.' He dredged up a smile, uncomfortable about admitting to what he considered a weakness. 'I know I should have got over it years ago, but sometimes it comes back to haunt me.'

'We're all the product of our upbringing, Mac.' She lifted his hand to her lips and pressed a kiss to his palm and her voice was so gentle, so tender that it brought a lump to his throat.

'Think so?' he murmured huskily.

'Oh, yes.' She smiled into his eyes. 'Look at me. My parents aren't demonstrative people and they didn't encourage me to show my feelings either. That's why I've always had such difficulty relating to other people—I tend to hold everything inside me rather than show how I really feel.'

'Really?' His brows rose and he grinned at her. 'I would never have guessed from the way you responded when we made love.'

'That was different,' she protested, a rush of colour staining her cheeks.

'Was it? Why?' He brushed her lips with the lightest of kisses, drawing back when he felt her immediately respond. His heart filled with joy, although he shouldn't assume that her response meant that it was *him* she wanted…

All of a sudden Mac couldn't wait any longer. Cupping her face between his hands, he looked into her eyes, knowing that this was the most important moment of his life. Whatever happened in the next few seconds was going to determine his whole future.

'Do you love me, Bella? I know I shouldn't put you on the spot like this, but I need to know before I drive myself crazy!'

* * *

Bella could feel her heart thumping. It was beating so hard that she could barely think, let alone answer the question. And then slowly through all the confusion in her head one thought rose to the surface. Of course she loved him. There was no doubt about that.

'Of course I love you,' she said indignantly, glaring at him. 'I'd have thought that was obvious.'

'Not to me.'

His voice was filled with a mixture of pure amazement and utter joy. Bella felt her indignation melt away as fast as it had appeared. Placing her hand on his cheek, she smiled at him, stunned by the fact that he was so vulnerable. Mac had always been so together, so in charge of himself—or so she had thought. To suddenly discover this whole different side to him was a revelation. She realised in that moment that she would do everything in her power to make sure that he never regretted letting her see the real man beneath the confident façade he presented to the world at large.

She kissed him softly on the mouth, letting her lips show him in no uncertain terms how she felt. She loved him so much and she wanted nothing more than to spend the rest of her days proving it to him…

If he would let her.

She drew back, feeling the first tiny doubt gnawing away at her happiness. Mac had asked her if she loved him. He had told her that he needed to know. However, he hadn't said why.

'I love you, Mac, but are you sure that you love me? You were so quick to think that I'd used you to clarify my feelings for Tim and you wouldn't have done that if you'd really loved me. You would have known that I would never have slept with you for that reason.'

It was the hardest thing Bella had ever done.

She had never done anything like this before, never delved into emotional issues, and it scared her to do it now when it was so important. Whatever Mac told her would affect the rest of her life and she wasn't sure if she could handle the thought.

She stood up abruptly, suddenly too afraid to sit there and listen to what he had to say. If Mac didn't want her then there was nothing she could do about it. She had to accept his decision and not make a scene, certainly not make a fool of herself by begging him to reconsider! Tears stung her eyes as she went to push past him but he was too quick for her. Reaching out, he drew her to a halt, his arms closing around her so that she couldn't move, couldn't escape him or the truth.

'Bella, stop! I know you're scared because I'm scared too, but you can't run away. I won't let you.' Bending, he pressed a kiss to her lips and she felt the shudder that passed through his body and into hers. Raising his head, he looked steadily at her. 'We both need to be brave if we're going to make this work. I love you and I want to spend my life with you. I think…*hope*…that you feel the same. Do you, my darling? Do you love me enough to live with me from now to eternity because I warn you that's what I want. Nothing less.'

Bella could feel her heart thumping. This was it. Whatever she said now would determine her future. Did she want to be with Mac for ever? Did she want to live with him and spend each and every day making him happy? Of course she did!

Reaching up, she drew his head down and kissed him, letting her lips answer his question. There was a moment when he held back, a tiny beat of time when he seemed to hesitate as though he wasn't sure that what was happening was real, and then he was kissing her back, kissing her with a hunger he didn't attempt to hide. They were both trembling when they broke apart, both shaken by the depth of their feelings for each other. Mac cupped her cheek and she could hear the love resonating in his voice.

'I didn't know it was possible to feel this way, Bella, to want someone *this* much.'

'Me neither.' Turning her head, she pressed a kiss against his palm and felt him shudder. It felt like the most natural thing in the world to tell him how she felt, to lay bare her emotions completely and totally. 'I want you so much that it hurts, Mac. I want to spend my life with you and spend every single second of every minute loving you. Even then it won't be enough. Nothing would be when I feel this way.'

'And you're sure? Sure that you want me and not Tim? After all, you agreed to meet him—'

'Yes, I did.' She laid her fingertips against his lips to silence him. 'And the reason I agreed was because of how I feel about you. I wanted to draw a line under past events and, if possible, make my peace with Tim. I want the future—our future, together—to be perfect and not tainted by anything that's happened in the past.'

'Oh, my love!'

He kissed her again, hunger replaced by a bone-melting tenderness that brought tears to her eyes. He smiled as he wiped them away with his fingertips. 'Don't cry, sweetheart. Although I have to confess that I feel very much like shedding a tear or two myself.'

'Just not right for your macho image,' she teased, smiling up at him through her tears.

'Definitely not. I should really be beating my chest right now, shouldn't I?' He grinned back at her. 'I mean, I've just won the woman I love and I should be celebrating before dragging you back to my cave.'

'Hmm. Let's not get too carried away by the

macho theme.' She laughed up at him. 'I'm a modern woman, after all, and I value my independence.'

'And so you should. I don't want you to change, Bella. I want you to stay exactly the same as you've always been.'

'I don't think that's possible,' she said quietly. 'I've changed a lot in the past few weeks and changed for the better too. I now understand my feelings and I'm not so afraid to show them, thanks to you. And, hopefully, I shall get even better at it as time passes too.'

'I've always thought you were perfect from the moment we met.'

His voice grated and Bella's eyes filled with tears once more because it was obvious that he was telling her the truth. Mac loved her exactly how she was and it was marvellous to know that he didn't want her to change. Reaching up, she kissed him, showing him without the need for words how much she loved him and how much she needed him. He'd said she was perfect but to her mind he was perfect too!

EPILOGUE

One year later...

MAC CAREFULLY LAID the baby in her crib. It was two a.m. and the rest of the town was sleeping. With a bit of luck, three-week-old Isobel Grace MacIntyre would follow suit.

'Has she dropped off at last?'

'Not yet.'

He turned, thinking that Bella had never looked more beautiful as she sat there propped against the pillows in their bed. They had married as soon as they had discovered that she was expecting the baby. He knew that they would have got married anyway but he had discovered that he was surprisingly old-fashioned in many ways and had wanted their child to be born in wedlock. The simple ceremony in the hospital's chapel had been perfect too, the final seal on their happiness, not that they had needed to prove it. He loved Bella with every fibre of his being, just as she loved him, and anyone could see how they felt too!

'I think she's debating whether or not to give her poor mum and dad a break.'

He lay down on the bed and gathered Bella into his arms, inhaling the warm womanly smell of her. She had decided to feed Isobel herself and he loved watching her do so, loved how her face filled with adoration for their baby, loved how fulfilled she looked with the infant nursing at her breast. Love, as he had discovered, was infinite and expanded on a daily basis.

He kissed her gently on the lips, drawing back when he felt his body immediately stir. It was too soon for them to make love because Bella needed time to heal after the birth. Anyway, waiting only made his desire for her even stronger, not that it hadn't been pretty strong to begin with!

'Mmm. I think I can guess what's on your mind,' she said, pulling back so she could look into his eyes, and he chuckled.

'Is it that obvious?'

'Yes.' She snuggled against him and sighed. 'Not just on your mind either.'

'Never mind. Just another couple of weeks and we can resume relations, as they say,' he said comfortingly, pulling her back to him.

'I can't wait,' she murmured against his chest. She suddenly drew back again. 'Did I tell you that I spoke to Freya this morning? Apparently, the results of her mock A-levels were so good that she's been offered a place at Lancaster. She will make a brilliant nurse, don't you think?'

'I do. I'm so glad that her parents saw sense in the end. She needs their support if she's to make a success of uni,' he said, pulling her back into his arms. He kissed the tip of her nose and smiled. 'Another set of grandparents who've been won over.'

'Like my parents, you mean.' She burrowed against him. 'Dad phoned as well this afternoon to let me know they're coming up to visit us at the weekend.'

'Again?' Mac laughed softly. 'That's the third time in as many weeks. Why do I get the feeling that they're going to turn into doting grandparents?'

'Oh, I've no idea, but don't knock it. Dad mentioned something about him and Mum babysitting if we wanted to go out for dinner. Sounds good to me.'

'Me too. So long as Isobel is all right, of course,' he added, glancing over at the crib.

'She'll be fine.' Bella snuggled even closer. 'Now, why don't we take advantage of the fact that she seems to have dropped off at last?'

'Mmm, sounds interesting. What do you suggest?' he asked, leering comically at her.

'I'm not sure. I shall leave that up to you.'

Mac laughed as he pulled her to him and kissed her hungrily. Maybe they couldn't make love just yet but there were other ways to show how they felt about one another. They just needed to be creative…

* * * * *

MILLS & BOON®
Large Print Medical

March

Falling at the Surgeon's Feet	Lucy Ryder
One Night in New York	Amy Ruttan
Daredevil, Doctor...Husband?	Alison Roberts
The Doctor She'd Never Forget	Annie Claydon
Reunited...in Paris!	Sue MacKay
French Fling to Forever	Karin Baine

April

The Baby of Their Dreams	Carol Marinelli
Falling for Her Reluctant Sheikh	Amalie Berlin
Hot-Shot Doc, Secret Dad	Lynne Marshall
Father for Her Newborn Baby	Lynne Marshall
His Little Christmas Miracle	Emily Forbes
Safe in the Surgeon's Arms	Molly Evans

May

A Touch of Christmas Magic	Scarlet Wilson
Her Christmas Baby Bump	Robin Gianna
Winter Wedding in Vegas	Janice Lynn
One Night Before Christmas	Susan Carlisle
A December to Remember	Sue MacKay
A Father This Christmas?	Louisa Heaton

MILLS & BOON®
Large Print Medical

June

Playboy Doc's Mistletoe Kiss	Tina Beckett
Her Doctor's Christmas Proposal	Louisa George
From Christmas to Forever?	Marion Lennox
A Mummy to Make Christmas	Susanne Hampton
Miracle Under the Mistletoe	Jennifer Taylor
His Christmas Bride-to-Be	Abigail Gordon

July

A Daddy for Baby Zoe?	Fiona Lowe
A Love Against All Odds	Emily Forbes
Her Playboy's Proposal	Kate Hardy
One Night...with Her Boss	Annie O'Neil
A Mother for His Adopted Son	Lynne Marshall
A Kiss to Change Her Life	Karin Baine

August

His Shock Valentine's Proposal	Amy Ruttan
Craving Her Ex-Army Doc	Amy Ruttan
The Man She Could Never Forget	Meredith Webber
The Nurse Who Stole His Heart	Alison Roberts
Her Holiday Miracle	Joanna Neil
Discovering Dr Riley	Annie Claydon

MILLS & BOON®
Large Print Medical

June

Playboy Doc's Mistletoe Kiss	Tina Beckett
Her Doctor's Christmas Proposal	Louisa George
From Christmas to Forever?	Marion Lennox
A Mummy to Make Christmas	Susanne Hampton
Miracle Under the Mistletoe	Jennifer Taylor
His Christmas Bride-to-Be	Abigail Gordon

July

A Daddy for Baby Zoe?	Fiona Lowe
A Love Against All Odds	Emily Forbes
Her Playboy's Proposal	Kate Hardy
One Night...with Her Boss	Annie O'Neil
A Mother for His Adopted Son	Lynne Marshall
A Kiss to Change Her Life	Karin Baine

August

His Shock Valentine's Proposal	Amy Ruttan
Craving Her Ex-Army Doc	Amy Ruttan
The Man She Could Never Forget	Meredith Webber
The Nurse Who Stole His Heart	Alison Roberts
Her Holiday Miracle	Joanna Neil
Discovering Dr Riley	Annie Claydon

MILLS & BOON®
Large Print Medical

March

Falling at the Surgeon's Feet	Lucy Ryder
One Night in New York	Amy Ruttan
Daredevil, Doctor...Husband?	Alison Roberts
The Doctor She'd Never Forget	Annie Claydon
Reunited...in Paris!	Sue MacKay
French Fling to Forever	Karin Baine

April

The Baby of Their Dreams	Carol Marinelli
Falling for Her Reluctant Sheikh	Amalie Berlin
Hot-Shot Doc, Secret Dad	Lynne Marshall
Father for Her Newborn Baby	Lynne Marshall
His Little Christmas Miracle	Emily Forbes
Safe in the Surgeon's Arms	Molly Evans

May

A Touch of Christmas Magic	Scarlet Wilson
Her Christmas Baby Bump	Robin Gianna
Winter Wedding in Vegas	Janice Lynn
One Night Before Christmas	Susan Carlisle
A December to Remember	Sue MacKay
A Father This Christmas?	Louisa Heaton

'Mmm, sounds interesting. What do you suggest?' he asked, leering comically at her.

'I'm not sure. I shall leave that up to you.'

Mac laughed as he pulled her to him and kissed her hungrily. Maybe they couldn't make love just yet but there were other ways to show how they felt about one another. They just needed to be creative…

* * * * *